MONSIEUR PAIN

ROBERTO BOLAÑO

MONSIEUR PAIN

Translated by Chris Andrews

A NEW DIRECTIONS BOOK

Originally published by Anagrama, Barcelona, Spain, as *Monsieur Pain* in 1999; published by arrangement with the Heirs of Roberto Bolaño and Carmen Balcells Agencia Literaria, Barcelona.

Manufactured in the United States of America
Published simultaneously in Canada by Penguin Books Canada, Ltd.
New Directions Books are printed on acid-free paper.
First published as a New Directions Book in 2010

Library of Congress Cataloging-in-Publication Data

Bolaño, Roberto, 1953–2003.
[Monsieur Pain. English]
[Monsieur Pain / Roberto Bolaño ; translated by Chris Andrews.
p. cm.
Originally published by Anagrama Barcelona Spain, as Monsieur Pain in 1999.
ISBN 978-0-8112-1714-9 (hardcover : alk. paper)
ISBN 978-0-8112-1889-4 (pbk. : alk. paper)
1. Vallejo, César, 1892–1938—Fiction. 2. Mesmerists—Fiction.
3. Mesmerism—Fiction. 4. Occultism—Fiction. 5. Unrequited love—Fiction. 6. Paris (France)—Fiction. I. Andrews, Chris, 1962–
II. Title.
PQ8098.12.038M6613 2010
863'.64—dc22   2009037431

10 9 8 7 6 5 4 3 2 1

New Directions Books are published for James Laughlin
by New Directions Publishing Corporation,
80 Eighth Avenue, New York 10011

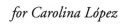

for Carolina López

P. Does the idea of death afflict you?

V. (Very quickly.) No–no!

P. Are you pleased with the prospect?

V. If I were awake I should like to die, but now it is no matter. The mesmeric condition is so near death as to content me.

P. I wish you would explain yourself, Mr Vankirk.

V. I am willing to do so, but it requires more effort than I feel able to make. You do not question me properly.

P. What then shall I ask?

V. You must begin at the beginning.

P. The beginning! But where is the beginning?

"Mesmeric Revelation"
Edgar Allan Poe

PRELIMINARY NOTE

Many years ago, in 1981 or 1982, I wrote *Monsieur Pain*. Its fate has been haphazard and erratic. Under the title *The Elephant Path* it won the Felix Urubayen prize for a short novel, awarded by the Toledo City Council. Not long before, it had been short-listed in another provincial competition, under a different title. I won three hundred thousand pesetas in Toledo. And around a hundred and twenty thousand in the other city, as I seem to recall. The Toledo City Council published the book and made me a judge for the following year. In the other provincial capital they forgot about me even sooner than I forgot about them, and I never found out whether or not the novel had been published there. All this is recounted in a story in *Last Evenings on Earth*. Time, that consummate joker, has subsequently sent a number of major prizes my way. But none of them has meant as much to me as those awards scattered over the map of Spain: buffalo prizes I had to go hunting like a redskin whose life is on the line. Never have I felt as proud or as wretched to be a writer. There's not a lot more I can say about *Monsieur Pain*. Almost all the events related actually occurred: Vallejo's hiccups, the carriage — a horse-drawn carriage — that ran over Curie, his last experiment, or one of his last, which touched on certain aspects of mesmerism, the doctors who were so negligent in their treatment of Vallejo. Even Pain is real. Georgette mentions him on a page of her passionate, bitter, helpless memoirs.

PARIS, 1938

On Wednesday the sixth of April, at dusk, as I was preparing to leave my lodgings, I received a telegram from my young friend Madame Reynaud, requesting, with a certain urgency, my presence that evening at the Café Bordeaux, on Rue de Rivoli, relatively close to where I live, which meant that if I hurried, I could still arrive punctually at the specified time.

The first indication that I had just been drawn into a singular episode presented itself immediately: as I was going down the stairs I came across two men climbing up to the third floor. They were speaking Spanish, a language I do not understand, and wearing dark trench-coats and broad-brimmed hats, which, since they were below me on the stairs, obscured their faces. Because of the semi-darkness that generally prevails in the stairwell, but also because of my quiet way of moving, they failed to notice my presence until I was right in front of them, a mere three steps away, at which point they stopped talking, and instead of stepping aside and allowing me to continue on my way down (the stairs are wide enough for two but not three people abreast), they looked at each other for a few moments that seemed to be fixed in a simulacrum of eternity (I should stress that I was a few steps above them), and then, slowly, very slowly, they trained their gazes on me. Policemen, I thought, only policemen have preserved that way of looking, an atavism that goes back to hunting and dark woods; then I remembered that they had been speaking Spanish, so they could not have belonged to the police force, or not the French police force, at any rate. I thought they were readying themselves to speak, to jabber as disoriented foreigners always do, but instead the one directly in front of me lurched aside in the clumsiest imaginable fashion, and pressed against the shoulder of his companion in a way that surely must have been uncomfortable for both of them, at which point, having pronounced a brief and unreciprocated greeting, I was able to continue my descent. Out of curiosity, when I reached the first-floor landing, I glanced back at them: they were still there, standing on the very same steps, I would swear, faintly illuminated by a globe suspended over the landing above them, and—even more surprisingly—still holding the exact position they had adopted in order to let me pass. As if time had stopped, I thought. When I reached the street I found it was raining, and I forgot all about that incident.

Madame Reynaud was seated against the far wall of the restaurant, her back held very straight, as usual. She seemed impatient, although when she caught sight of me her expression softened, as if a sudden relaxation were the appropriate manner in which to indicate that she had recognized me and was waiting.

"I want you to see the husband of a friend of mine," was the first thing she said, as soon as I took my place in front of her, facing an enormous wall-mirror, in which the restaurant could be surveyed almost in its entirety.

Guided by some recondite analogy, I remembered the face of her young husband, who had died not long before.

"Pierre," she repeated, stressing each word, "you must see my friend's husband, professionally, it's urgent."

I think I ordered a glass of mint cordial before asking what illness Monsieur . . .

"Vallejo," said Madame Reynaud, adding, with equal concision, "Hiccups."

I don't know why fragmentary images of a face, which could have been the face of the late Monsieur Reynaud, superimposed themselves on the people drinking and chatting at the nearby tables.

"Hiccups?" I asked with a sad smile that was intended to be respectful.

"He's dying," my interlocutor affirmed vehemently. "No one knows why; it's no joke. You have to save his life."

"I'm afraid," I whispered, as she looked out the front window, nervously watching the flow of passers-by on Rue de Rivoli, "I'm afraid that if you can't be more explicit . . ."

"I'm not a doctor, Pierre, I don't understand these things, it's something I deeply regret, as you know; I always wanted to be a nurse." Her blue eyes shone furiously. It was true that Madame Reynaud had not pursued advanced studies (in fact she had not pursued any studies at all), but that did not prevent me from considering her a woman of lively intelligence.

Frowning slightly and lowering her eyelashes, with the intonation of someone reciting a text learned by heart, she added:

"Monsieur Vallejo has been in hospital since the end of

March. The doctors still don't know what's wrong, but one thing is clear: he's dying. Yesterday he began to suffer from the hiccups . . ." She stopped for a moment and looked around at the people in the restaurant, as if attempting to locate someone. "That is, yesterday he began hiccupping constantly and no one has been able to do anything to help him. As you know, in extreme cases, hiccups can be fatal. As if that weren't enough, he's running a temperature of more than forty degrees. Madame Vallejo, whom I've known for years, called me this morning. She's alone, with no one to turn to except her husband's friends, who are almost all South Americans. When she explained her situation, I thought of you, although of course I didn't promise her anything."

"I'm honored by your confidence," I managed to whisper.

"I have faith in you," she replied immediately

Faith is the first requirement for love, I thought. She looked fragile. Her eyes were dry (why should they not have been?) and seemed to be unhurriedly studying the shoulders of my jacket.

"You can succeed where the doctors have failed, with acupuncture."

She put her hand on mine; I felt a faint tremor; for a moment, Madame Reynaud's fingers seemed transparent.

"Believe me, you are the only person who can save my friend's husband, but we must hurry; if you accept, you will have to see Vallejo tomorrow."

"How could I refuse?" I said, not daring to look at her.

"I knew it!" Her cry caught the attention of the people sitting around us: "Oh, Pierre, I believe in you, I really do!"

"What should I do first?" I asked, cutting her off, and noticing in the mirror that my face was flushed, with pleasure perhaps, while over by the till, two tall, thin, hollow-cheeked individuals dressed in black were engaged in conversation with the waiter, as if they were settling their bill or confiding in him.

"I don't know, Pierre, I need to speak with Georgette, with Madame Vallejo," she said, "and arrange a time to-morrow, as early as possible."

"I quite agree. The sooner I can gauge the condition of your friend's husband, the better," I declared.

The waiter and the two men in black turned to look at us. The men, who were extremely pale, nodded their heads in unison, as if to signal assent. I was momentarily under the strange impression that those men, the pair of them, were one of the possible incarnations of pity. I wondered if Madame Reynaud might know them.

"They're watching us."

"Who?"

"Over there, next to the till—don't look straight away—two men in black. They look like a pair of angels, don't you think?"

"Nonsense! Truly, Pierre! Angels are young and rosy-cheeked. Those poor men look like they just came out of jail."

"Or out of a cellar."

"Although they're probably just tired office workers, or ill, perhaps."

"True. Do you know them?"

"No, of course not," she replied, her eyes fixed on my tie-pin.

She seemed to have shrunk.

•   •   •

Six months earlier, in spite of my efforts, Madame Reynaud's husband had died, at the age of twenty-four. Exactly a week before that, Madame Reynaud had appeared at the door of my apartment with a brief letter of introduction from old Monsieur Rivette, a mutual friend, and from the very start I had known that there was nothing I could do; the doctors had long since declared the patient beyond recovery, and it was clear that only someone as young and as desperate as Madame Reynaud could have persisted in the hope that they were mistaken. Breaking with my customary practice, and, I must admit, somewhat wearily, I acceded to her pleas. That day I visited Monsieur Reynaud, who was lying on his deathbed at the Hôpital de la Salpêtrière, which I had been visiting for some years already, since a number of doctors there, who held me in high regard, would call from time to time upon my elementary knowledge of acupuncture to aid them in various courses of treatment.

Monsieur Reynaud had a swarthy complexion and dark green eyes—a southerner, it seemed—and was gracefully pretending to be unaware of his state of health. I took to him immediately: he was handsome and awkward and one only had to spend five minutes in his company to understand his wife's devotion.

"They're all crazy if they think I'm going to recover," he confessed to me the second night, after I had recounted certain trivial details of my daily routine, to distract him, and perhaps to create a space of mutual trust.

"Don't think like that." I smiled.

"You don't understand, Pain." His face was slightly turned toward me and it shone, but his eyes were searching for something that I couldn't see.

I stayed with him until he died.

"You shouldn't blame yourself, we all knew it was inevitable," said Doctor Durand that night, trying to console me.

From then on I began seeing Madame Reynaud every two or three weeks. Was it friendship? I don't know. Perhaps it was something more, although when we met it was usually just to go for a walk and pass the time chatting about this and that, never broaching our feelings or political convictions, or at least not hers; I did almost all the talking, and much to my regret the conversations tended to revolve around my already somewhat distant youth, the Great War, in which I had fought, my interest in the occult sciences, and our common love of cats. It is true that we also went to the movies, always at my request, or took refuge in restaurants, wherever our steps had led us, and generally sat there in silence. A silence that comforted both of us. There was never the slightest allusion to matters of an intimate or emotional nature, except perhaps on those occasions when Madame Reynaud quite innocently took me into her confidence and spoke of her late husband. And finally, we never visited each other at home (except for that first time, when Madame Reynaud came to find me with the letter of introduction from Monsieur Rivette), although we had each other's addresses.

Unhurriedly, as I walked home, I began to recompose Monsieur Reynaud's fever-stricken face, while meditating on the hiccups afflicting Monsieur Vallejo, with whom I was still unacquainted. A recurring image, it occurred to me: during the preceding months I had found it difficult not to associate illness and even beauty with the memory of Monsieur Reynaud. It was almost midnight. After leaving Madame Reynaud I had spent the remainder of the evening in a café in Passy with an old acquaintance, a retired tailor who devoted the better part of his time to the study of mesmerism. The rain had stopped. It struck me that the deep secrets of a condition are often revealed by the person who brings us into contact with the patient. The intermediary as a kind of X-ray. As a theory, it was, of course, highly speculative, and I gave it little credence. What had Madame Reynaud revealed about my future patient? Nothing. All she had revealed was her own morbid curiosity about my competence. That is, she wanted to see me cure someone, finally, and so justify the trust she had placed in me. My role and mission when I first appeared in her life had been to save her husband, and I had failed, but now I had a second chance, with her friend's husband; I had to save him, and so testify to a higher reality, a logical order, in which we could continue to be who we were. And perhaps come to recognize one another, finally, and having attained that recognition, change, and, in my case, aspire to happiness. (A reasonable happiness, akin to care and trust.) And yet there was something amiss, something I could sense in Madame Reynaud's silences and the state of my own sensory apparatus, which was on the alert, although I couldn't tell why. An extraordinary malaise was lurking in the most trivial details. I believe I sensed the danger, but had no notion of its nature.

Suddenly, as I turned the corner into my street, which is normally deserted at that time of night, my fears were vindicated by the sound of quickening steps. I walked on a few yards before stopping, in shock. I am being followed, I realized, with a blend of certitude and astonishment, like a soldier discovering that gangrene has taken hold of his leg. Was it possible?

Cautiously, I glanced over my shoulder; two men were walking abreast behind me at a distance of about twenty yards, so close together they seemed to be Siamese twins, wearing enormous broad-brimmed hats, their black silhouettes standing out against the light shed by a lamp on the other side of the street.

I knew that as they walked, they were keeping their eyes fixed on me. So intense was the sensation of being observed that it triggered a physical pain, a pain that turned me into someone else. I covered the remaining distance to my apartment building as quickly as I could. I can't remember hearing them run, which leads me to think that my reaction took them by surprise. Once inside, having managed to close the hall door, I found that I was sweating profusely. With my back against the door, I thought: Perspiration is an unequivocal sign of good health. Later I felt deeply ashamed; I must have run, I thought, and the men must have supposed, with good reason, that I was running from them, and so on. Just as this bout of self-reproach, which had only served to humiliate me, was coming to an end, just as I was catching my breath in preparation for the steep climb up to the fifth floor, I heard two voices on the other side of the door, more or less at ear level, jabbering in Spanish.

I climbed the stairs as quietly as possible, without switching on the light, and shut myself in my room. Having lit the gas ring and made myself a cup of tea, I got into bed and said to myself that my daily routines were bound to be disturbed by the new elements that had entered my life since the previous day. Movement, I thought. The circle opens at the most unexpected point. I have a patient who is dying of the hiccups; two Spaniards are clearly following me (and my patient, although not Spanish, is Latin American); Madame Reynaud behaved nervously when she saw the two tall gentlemen who were watching us in the Café Bordeaux; they are not the Spaniards who have been following me, but Madame Reynaud seemed to know (or guess) who they were and to be afraid of them.

April, I thought. A new life-phase. At some point I fell asleep.

I woke late, with a headache. Someone was knocking at the door. It was Madame Grenelle, who rents the rooms adjoining mine, holding two standard paper envelopes, one blue, one white, pinched between finger and thumb. When she saw me she stifled a cry:

"Monsieur Pain, you gave me such a fright!"

"But all I did was open the door," I said, in fact, the way I had opened it, far from being abrupt, was almost too slow, as if I were *resigned*. And Madame Grenelle had taken fright!

"It's midday," she said, craning her neck in the vain hope of finding an overnight companion in my lodgings.

To preserve my dignity, I half closed the door and asked if the letters were for me.

"Of course," she said, "nobody writes to me; the only letters I ever get are from the provinces, from my sister or my late husband's sister, never from anyone in Paris."

She smiled defiantly, her double chin at the level of my chest. I tried to smile too, understandingly.

"They were delivered in person. This one," she waved the white envelope like a fan, "by two foreigners, Spaniards or Italians. And this one," she flourished the blue envelope delicately, with a complicit wink, "by a courier. But smell it. Can you smell the perfume?"

I remained impassive, feigning disinterest, with my hands in the pockets of my dressing-gown, staring off into the cold, deserted hallway.

"Did you see the foreign gentlemen?"

"Yes, and I spoke with the courier too, a poor boy just up from Albi, who doesn't even know his way around the city."

"Did you speak with the Spaniards?"

"Were they Spaniards?"

"I believe so," I said rather uncertainly. "Did you speak with them?"

"A little. They were knocking at your door for a long time, it must have been around nine. You are a heavy sleeper, Monsieur Pain."

"What did they say, Madame Grenelle?"

"Nothing in particular. They asked me if you lived here and I said yes, of course, but that you must have spent the night somewhere else; who would have guessed you were in bed? Then they asked me if you often spent the night elsewhere and I said that it was none of my business, although I did assure them that you were not a man of bohemian habits, but a scholar, and very rarely away overnight. They clearly found it hard to understand me, or didn't know how to reply. Anyway, they stood there quietly, as if waiting to hear a noise from your room, then one of them wrote a note, put it in an envelope and gave it to me; the envelope is sealed, see. He kept saying that it had to be given to you without delay, it was urgent. He went on and on. All right, all right, I said, I understand, don't worry. The other one kept his ear to the door; I think he still hadn't given up hope."

Mumbling a few words of thanks, I seized the letters and closed the door. Then, as I heard Madame Grenelle's footsteps receding down the hallway, I remembered waking from a dream at some point during the night, a dream in which a person who wished me well (that much I could dimly sense) was covering my mouth in a gentle but determined and authoritative way. I woke to find my own hand pressed against my lips. As if I were trying to suffocate myself? As if I were trying to stop myself from speaking?

Sitting on the edge of the bed, I opened the white envelope: *Monsieur Pierre Pain, your presence is requested at the Café Victor, in the Latin Quarter, at 10 pm. It is a matter of the utmost gravity. Do not ignore this request.* There was no signature, of course. The blue envelope was from Madame Reynaud and the message read as follows: *Dear friend, I have spoken with Madame Vallejo and arranged for the three of us to meet today, at 4 pm in the Café Bordeaux. Monsieur Vallejo's condition is unchanged; he is still hiccupping and his fever has not abated. Madame Vallejo does not anticipate any difficulty with the doctor who is treating her husband. Nor do I. Yours, Marcelle Reynaud.*

I looked at the façade of the clinic through the slightly fogged window of the taxi and understood that what lay behind it, more than anything, even more than madness, was solitude, which is perhaps the subtlest or at least the most lucid of the forms that madness can take.

It was seven in the evening on the seventh of April, and

Madame Vallejo, Madame Reynaud and I had just arrived at the Clinique Arago. I had barely spoken during the taxi ride. The women seemed to have a great deal to say to each other, and in any case my thoughts had strayed into nebulous regions that were hardly compatible with chatting.

"You seem miles away," remarked Madame Reynaud, while at the other end of the lobby, her friend exchanged a few words with the nurse in charge of reception.

"Not at all," I replied with a smile.

Then we followed Madame Vallejo down grey and white corridors, with a metallic, phosphorescent sheen, blemished here and there by unexpected black rectangles.

"It's like a modern art gallery," I heard Madame Reynaud murmur.

"The corridors are circular, in fact," I said. "If they were longer we could reach the top story without ever having noticed the climb."

"Like the leaning tower of Pisa," commented Madame Vallejo.

It was not an apt analogy, but I didn't want to contradict her.

Madame Reynaud smiled at me strangely: the hospital's atmosphere was saddening her, giving her face a serious and expectant look.

"It's all so white," she said.

"It's unnatural," added Madame Vallejo, taking her by the arm and hurrying on.

I followed them.

The two friends were walking quickly but their steps were unsteady. Watching them from behind I had the impression that the heels of their shoes were loose. I put it all down to nerves. I also noticed that the lighting in the corridors, contrived in a cunning but mysterious manner, since the illumination extended uniformly even into corners where the newcomer could see no trace of wiring or globes, was however varying in intensity; almost imperceptibly, at regular intervals, it dimmed.

Suddenly we came across a man in a white coat, the first we had seen in the course of our exploration, standing stock still in the middle of the corridor and apparently plunged in deep cogitations. As we approached, he raised his eyes, sizing us up with his lips curved in a mocking grin, and crossed his arms. He gave an impression of coldness, or at least that is what I thought at the time. At any rate, it was evident from his expression that our sudden appearance had displeased him. Madame Vallejo slowed her pace noticeably, as if to delay the inevitable encounter with that man. Clearly they knew one another and she was afraid of him. But why?

We were formally introduced:

"Doctor Lejard, my husband's GP."

Lejard greeted us with a nod but did not utter a word, not even when the reason for my visit was explained to him. He was focusing his attention, in a conspicuous and rather studied manner, on Madame Reynaud.

I remained silent, scrutinizing the doctor's lean face, while Madame Vallejo said something about urine tests that had not been carried out, or perhaps the results had gone astray; Lejard, in any case, simply shrugged. Later, when I felt that the moment to speak had come, I addressed him directly, asking with ill-disguised innocence what illness, in his opinion, Monsieur Vallejo was suffering from. His cutting reply was proffered in a baritone voice:

"I'm not obliged to answer that question. Ask Madame Vallejo. She's aware of the latest developments; I'm not. I've never had much time for charlatans, personally."

"What . . . " stammered Madame Vallejo.

Madame Reynaud took her by the arm.

"Georgette . . ."

Ignoring the women, Lejard stared at me and smiled, as if giving me time to digest what he had flung in my face. Beside me, Madame Vallejo was blushing visibly; her jaw was tense and she seemed to be about to slap the doctor. I simply sighed, vainly attempting to assume a nonchalant expression, and examined the outlines of my shoes.

As Lejard walked away, after a perfunctory salute, which turned up the corners of his ironic smile, the three of us must have formed a peculiar tableau: frozen in the hallway, dumbstruck, unable to utter even a banal remark to break the silence, our faces turned toward a space no longer occupied by anyone, as if we were expecting Lejard to materialize exactly there and proceed to excuse himself. I can confidently say that my two companions felt the humiliation far more keenly than I did. The doctor's attitude, though particularly malicious in this case, was not unfamiliar to me.

I coughed a couple of times, looking away from the women, sensing that they would prefer not to be watched, and we were about to resume our journey when, all of a sudden, before we had time to react, a mass of figures dressed in white advanced toward us, like an avalanche unleashed by a snowball.

When they reached us, a man with messy hair and moist eyes stepped forward and took Madame Vallejo by the arm, crying:

"The eminent Doctor Lemière is here."

His words resonated as if in a church. The light dimmed again and my hair bristled: he had simply trotted out his ritual phrase.

Confirming the assertion, a plump little man in the middle of the group smiled to the left and the right, called for silence by raising his hand, which he then stretched out, with some difficulty until it reached the gloved hand of Madame Vallejo.

"A pleasure to meet you. I have just seen your husband. All his organs are in perfect working order! I can't see what's wrong with the man. May I?"

Madame Vallejo followed Doctor Lemière, who led her by the elbow to a door which hid the corridor's spiral curvature. From where I was standing, they were shrunken, childlike figures. Doctor Lemière's white mane, matching the double door behind him, was animated by a series of small jerks, marking affirmations, negations and questions; Madame Vallejo's head moved only once, turning briefly, searching for us in vain, as if to say good-bye.

"We'd better go," whispered Madame Reynaud.

The doctors accompanying Lemière looked at us with weary, flat eyes, devoid of hope. It was as if I had somehow become the invisible man. A tall handsome young fellow was whispering in the ear of a dark, plump girl with an intelligent face. Another young man was holding a notebook and staring up at the roof. Behind him three others stood quietly and calmly with their hands in their pockets; to their left, a blond boy was looking intently at the palm of one of his hands and holding an extinguished cigarette in the other. With his back to the blond boy, the man who had introduced Lemière and who presumably belonged to the clinic's administrative staff was listening to the chatter of a bald fellow with an abundant moustache, who was standing very close to him and clasping at least four massive tomes with cracked spines.

Two members of the group, standing apart from the

others, almost against the opposite wall of the hallway, struck me as familiar. Both were wearing stethoscopes around their necks.

"But I must see Monsieur Vallejo," I protested softly. The volume of my voice was so low, I couldn't tell if I had spoken or merely thought.

"Not now. Follow me. I'll explain outside."

Madame Reynaud's blue eyes seemed drained of life; it's the whiteness, I thought, that artificial light. I was about to follow her when I noticed a slight fissure in the scene: there was a trace of alarm in the faces of the two familiar-seeming doctors. I smiled in their direction, perhaps expecting them to respond with a gesture and confirm my supposition, but they maintained an impassivity perfectly matching that of their colleagues. I walked away, following Madame Reynaud. I remember she outpaced me; with every heavy step I took, I felt as if my legs were made of lead. In the end I stopped. The sensation of being in an art gallery spread through my veins and paralyzed me. Madame Reynaud kept walking. I looked back; Madame Vallejo had taken off a glove and was glancing back and forth between her nails and Lemière's face. My position, equidistant from both women, must have betrayed confusion and awkwardness, but no one was paying me any attention. At that moment, as if by design, the lights in the hallway flickered. I thought, Now there really will be a blackout. Madame Reynaud's shadow seemed to crash into the wall. I turned my head again: some of the doctors were looking up at the ceiling listlessly, as if the phenomenon were not unfamiliar to them. The intensity of the illumination, once it stabilized, was considerably reduced. Now the hallway was bathed in a dim sepia light and the shadows stretched off indistinctly. Madame Reynaud was waiting for me at the other end of the corridor with her lips slightly parted, as if she had pronounced an inaudible word—my name perhaps. For the last time I turned my gaze to the group of doctors. The two I thought I knew were still there, set apart somehow, like foreign students, I thought.

The word *foreign* gave me the key; I understood then who they were and where I had seen them, and I ran to Madame Reynaud, who looked at me in surprise.

"Monsieur Pain, remember that we are in a hospital," she said to me reprovingly.

Outside it had begun to rain: a fine drizzle, which though barely noticeable intensified the lonely stillness of the night. Madame Reynaud had brought an umbrella. The street was empty, as if the inhabitants of the neighborhood had all chosen to stay in their apartments. I did, however, note the following detail: the street lamps were the only sources of light. Were there people in the unlit apartments? We walked along the sidewalk arm in arm. All of a sudden, I don't know why, everything seemed perfect. Madame Reynaud's profile, the dripping of the rain on the umbrella, the sense of adventure, faint but shared.

"Doctor Lemière is a famous specialist, at least that is what Madame Vallejo told me yesterday. As it happens, just yesterday she was telling me how difficult it was, impossible in fact, to get the clinic's leading physician to take an interest in her husband's case. Someone must have put in a word for Monsieur Vallejo and finally convinced Lemière to make some room in his busy schedule. An odd coincidence, though, don't you think? But it was exactly what Madame Vallejo had been hoping for. So, you see, we were rather in the way."

"What you mean is that Lemière wouldn't tolerate *my*

presence in his patient's room," I protested. "The doctor and the quack are incompatible."

"I didn't say that, Monsieur Pain. And anyway, you're not a quack."

"That's how I was treated. Have you forgotten already?"

"The business with Lejard? Are you cross about that?"

"No . . ."

"Well, stop frowning then. And watch your step, you just put your foot in a puddle."

In fact I was happy. The rain, the night, Madame Reynaud's scolding: the simplest things bring happiness.

"And what does it have to do with Doctor Lejard anyway?"

"Lejard is still Monsieur Vallejo's doctor. All Lemière can do is give a second opinion, but that's a considerable improvement on the previous situation."

"To judge from what I saw, Lejard is not on particularly good terms with Madame Vallejo."

"Nor with Monsieur Vallejo, as I understand."

"Why not change doctors then?"

"Because it's not up to them, my friend. Between you and me, Lejard let four days go by without visiting Vallejo. What do you think of that?"

"It's appalling."

"The problem is, the Vallejos have no money. Monsieur Vallejo's admission was organized by a certain Monsieur García Calderón, one of his compatriots, who also arranged for his personal doctor, that is, Lejard, to take on the case."

"When was he admitted?"

"The twenty-fourth of March."

"It's odd, I thought I recognized two of the doctors in Lemière's group of followers, but I must have been mistaken; the men I was thinking of are foreigners, Spaniards, I believe, and to tell the truth, it's hard to imagine them as doctors or medical students. They're more like gangsters in training. But they're not in the least frightening," I hastened to add.

"What do they look like?"

"Thin, dark . . . I don't think they're familiar with the city. They're enjoying themselves, don't ask me how I know. I really couldn't say. I just have the impression they like to live it up."

"I'm not aware of any Spanish doctor having seen Monsieur Vallejo. There's a Peruvian doctor who comes regularly. Monsieur Vallejo is Peruvian, did I tell you?"

At precisely ten o'clock at night, having taken my leave of Madame Reynaud at the entrance to a metro station, I arrived at the Café Victor, on Boulevard Saint Michel. My name was written in the headwaiter's notebook, and I was guided without delay to one of the private rooms where the Spaniards awaited me. Although the restaurant's lighting was in no way deficient or abnormal, I had the impression, on stepping inside, that I was entering a dark movie theater after the beginning of the show, preceded by the waiter, who for the occasion had been transformed into an usher guiding me to my seat. The bat, I thought. The path that links the man who serves and the man who sees in the dark.

"You're punctual," said one of the Spaniards.

I froze, with my hat in my hands, on the near side of the private room's blood-colored door. It was difficult to recognize them without their white coats, but it was clear that the two doctors I had noticed among Lemière's followers and the two Spaniards I had encountered on the stairs, who had come back the next morning to leave a message, were the same pair of men.

"A glass of wine?" asked the thinner of the two, patiently filling the third glass on the table up to the brim.

I sat down in front of them, as close to the door as I could, putting off the explanations that I should have been demanding.

"This must seem rather strange to you, I know, but it's not," said the other man, smiling; he was darker, although, to be honest I should say that both of them were thin and dark, and disturbingly, at certain moments, those were their *sole* characteristics.

My hand shook as I picked up the glass; a large portion of its contents spilled onto the tablecloth.

"We really just wanted to talk with you; don't worry about the cloth, it doesn't matter."

"A chat among friends, if you'll allow me to be so familiar."

"An informal chat."

"But drink, drink up, we've ordered some food, nothing special, cold cuts to snack on, we can go and have dinner somewhere else afterwards."

"I'm vegetarian," was the first thing I said.

The Spaniards looked at each other in surprise—or feigning surprise, perhaps—and then smiled indulgently, as if I had told a feeble joke and they were forgiving me.

"Gaston," one of them called out when the waiter came in with two platters covered with slices of ham, little sections of sparerib and various kinds of cheese. "Bring walnuts and almonds for our guest."

I tried to protest but he stopped me with a pale, wrinkled hand.

"Don't forget the peanuts, Gaston," he said when the waiter had already disappeared.

The dark one loosened his tie and smiled at me; his companion had fallen on one of the platters and was swallowing large chunks of cheese and washing them down with wine in the most indecorous manner.

"To be frank, gentlemen," I said, holding the glass up to my nose, as if I were smelling the contents, "I didn't come here to eat."

The Spaniards laughed heartily, and not in a malicious way; the one who was eating spluttered, raised his glass to me, and busied himself with the platters again.

"Actually," said the dark one, "I have no idea what the waiter's called; we call them all Gaston, and if one of us is right, if the waiter really is called Gaston, the other one has to pay for the meal, you see?"

"No, I don't. No one can win with that system." The dark one looked at me, perplexed. "If you and your friend both call all the waiters Gaston, you obviously both win or both lose. One of you should call them Gaston and the other . . . Raoul."

The dark one thought for a moment, then nodded several times.

"You're right. Maybe our system is too perfect. You must have read Newton, of course."

I didn't answer.

"We know you're thinking of treating Vallejo," said the thin one sadly.

I observed him through the glass of wine: a slow, red eel, sucking his teeth and drinking with a feigned parsimony.

"Was that why you were following me last night?"

"We went to your apartment to find you, twice," he said with an obsequious smile. "We know where you live, Monsieur Pain. Why would we need to follow you?"

"True, but if it wasn't you, it must have been two of your compatriots."

"When?" He appeared to be genuinely interested.

"Last night, after our encounter on the stairs."

For a few seconds the Spaniards appeared to be lost in thought.

"Well . . . but that's irrelevant, isn't it? Just a coincidence, because it certainly wasn't us." He didn't sound very convinced. "Anyway, let's get to the heart of the matter."

"The heart of the matter?"

"The common good," he said. "Or common sense, if you prefer."

The dark one swallowed a pair of pills that he had taken from a little nickel-plated box. The box was almost flat and transformed the light striking it into curious reflected figures. I had never seen such an object. I was relieved when he put it back into the inside pocket of his jacket.

"As I'm sure you've already guessed," he said, "we want you to forget all about it: Vallejo, his wife, us, everything."

I put my lips to the rim of the glass. I couldn't think. The situation was bizarre to say the least. I mustn't lose control, I thought. I drank. A long gulp in the vain hope of calming myself.

"Our request," the last word was stressed, "does not of course imply any lack of respect for your capabilities. On the contrary, I can assure you, and my companion will vouch for me, that I greatly admire the expertise you have demonstrated in your field. A very broad field it is, too, and I dare say quite unfamiliar to the majority of mortals, am I right?"

I nodded, and immediately felt contemptible.

"But you have no business with Vallejo. For the common good."

"The common good," the other sighed, "a nice definition, your good and the good of all . . . Harmony . . . Balance . . . The stability of the spheres . . . The tunnels filled again . . . Smiles . . ."

I was going to object that I didn't understand a word of that gibberish, but on second thoughts I felt that it would be better to remain silent. Leaning against the chair's vermilion backrest, the dark one kept his eyes fixed on me, but his gaze was curious rather than threatening. He was studying me. I don't know why, but this lifted my spirits. On a mad impulse, I refilled my glass and drank, almost hopefully.

"Was it Lejard who sent you?"

"That is a question we are not going to answer," sighed the thin one. "In fact, to be totally frank with you, we are not going to answer any questions unless they are absolutely essential to the satisfactory conclusion of our agreement with you."

"Agreement?"

"We've already told you: you forget about the existence of Vallejo, the Clinique Arago and the rest, and we'll forget about this envelope."

Lazily, but also with an artificial, studied arrogance, the dark one took out a long, dark-brown envelope, of the kind used by the Bank of Paris ten years ago, and dropped it onto the table beside the bottle. It contained more than two thousand francs.

"But why?"

The thin one raised a warning finger and traced a hieroglyph in the air, keeping me at a distance.

"No questions, remember."

It was obvious that although they had witnessed the encounter between Lemière and Madame Vallejo that afternoon, the Spaniards were still unaware that I no longer had any involvement in the case. Lemière had taken charge of everything, along with his medical team and Lejard; it was idiotic to pay me to wash my hands of something from which I had, in any case, been excluded. The chords of a tango were faintly audible in the distance. The crystalline laughter of a woman. I heard a master of ceremonies saying: "Alan Monardes in person will play for you . . ."

"This is madness."

"All right, but it's not going to do you any harm. On the contrary, the way things are going, a little bit of money put aside could come in very handy . . ."

They're mad, I thought, but the money is real, and it was there, waiting to be taken and slipped into my wallet. For the first time I was not afraid.

"This is the strangest bribe I've ever heard of," I murmured. Of course they didn't understand.

The thin one smiled, letting it pass.

"Let's call Gaston," he said as he rang the bell, "and order another bottle of wine. The night is still young."

The dark one corrected him: "The night is always young."

• • •

"Monsieur Rivette?"

"Ah, Pierre Pain."

"I'm calling from Raoul's café, it must be very late."

"It doesn't matter, don't worry, I wasn't asleep."

"I think I'm drunk. I needed . . . to speak with someone I can trust, dear Monsieur Rivette."

"Tell me how I can help you."

"This evening I did something vile and repugnant . . ."

" . . ."

"I accepted a bribe."

"You?"

"I know, it's hard to believe that anyone in the world would want to bribe a poor devil like me."

"That's not what I meant, Pierre—calm down, you sound very nervous."

"And how often have you known me to be nervous, Monsieur Rivette? Think about it . . ."

"That's beside the point, Pierre, human nature is unfathomable. Do you remember Pleumeur-Bodou?"

"What was that?"

"Pleumeur-Bodou."

"My god, I haven't thought of him in years. I suppose we were friends, once."

"The will to forget. Magic. Pleumeur-Bodou wasn't the nervous type, was he? Do you remember?"

"Didn't he commit suicide?"

"No. He's been living in Spain for more than a year. Every now and then I get a letter from him. He enjoys reminiscing about the old days."

"Well I don't. Or not much. I prefer to accept or tolerate myself as I am now. But why did you mention Pleumeur-Bodou?"

"I don't know, I suppose I must have been thinking about him . . . and about you."

"Today?"

"All afternoon. You know how it is, old folks like me, we like to revisit times gone by. I was looking at an astrological chart I drew up for both of you."

"For Pleumeur-Bodou and me? You never told me."

"It was nothing really. Don't worry about it. Anyway, what were you saying about a bribe?"

"I took it. I let them corrupt me."

"Do you mean you took money?"

"Exactly. They gave me two thousand francs and got me drunk. Then we were subjected to a performance by some wretched tango orchestra and went on drinking. I even ate meat! A juicy Argentinean steak!"

"Pierre . . ."

"And I wasn't being forced. I wanted to know. That's why I stayed: out of curiosity. In fact, my dear Monsieur Rivette, they paid me not to do something that I already knew I couldn't do anyway. But they didn't know that. What they did know, however, and hours, it seems, before I was informed myself, was that I would be asked to treat the patient in question. Hours before, do you see?"

" . . ."

"Hours before I was even aware of my ex-patient's existence, they tried to find me and stop me from taking on the case. I say *ex-* but he was never really my patient at all. I have never even seen him! But they knew, and took the necessary steps. It's as if they had planned an ambush and were lurking at a bend in the road, but I have never walked that road and never will. How would you explain that?"

"There are explanations for everything, Pierre, except

the inexplicable; remember Terzeff, that poor boy who claimed to have refuted Madame Curie."

"Terzeff . . . wasn't he Pleumeur-Bodou's friend?"

"Exactly. He was the scientist, although Pleumeur-Bodou was just as clever. A brilliant young man, Terzeff, or so he seemed, at first. None of his theories, of course, could be proved."

"It must be the alcohol, I can't remember anything, I haven't drunk so much in ages."

"There was a love affair behind it all, do you remember? Terzeff was in love with Madame Curie's daughter, Irène, and that was why he tried to prove her mother wrong, I always thought."

"Terzeff was the one who killed himself, wasn't he?"

"Exactly, he hung himself from the Pont Mirabeau, one night in 1925 . . . I think it was in winter, January or February . . . terrible days."

"God, it's laughable, isn't it, Monsieur Rivette. It's all so sad and absurd: Terzeff in love with Irène Joliot-Curie, me bothering you at this hour of the night."

"I wasn't asleep, my friend, I was reading—you could say I was waiting for your call—at our age, as you know, a few hours of sleep are enough."

"For Raoul too, it seems. He has shut the café, and now he's playing solitaire at one of the tables."

"Solitaire?"

"Yes . . . he's sitting in the middle of the café, two tables away from the bar, trying to finish a game of solitaire."

"A disturbing scene, my dear Pierre."

"No . . . not really . . ."

" . . ."

"At the back of the café there's someone else, behind the bar, sitting on a stool next to a door that leads god knows where. It's Raoul's wife, she must be doing the day's accounts or reading a novel. Anyhow, what were we talking about?"

"About you, Pierre, and that curious bribe."

"Shameful is what you mean."

"No, no, no . . . think of it as a consequence of your curiosity."

"But I accepted the money. Two thousand francs."

"There was clearly a misunderstanding and you took advantage of it."

"Shamefully, contemptibly, like a pimp . . ."

"You can return the money and that will put an end to the matter."

"I thought I had nothing to lose, my professional ethics didn't even come into it. Professional ethics! The ethics of the oldest profession, maybe. What I thought was: I need the money! I'm sorry."

" . . . "

"Now I wouldn't even know where to find the Spaniards. I saw them this afternoon at the Clinique Arago, but I don't think they work there. I don't know why, but for some reason I'm sure they don't work there . . . Have you been to the Clinique Arago?"

"No."

"It's a nightmare. The hallways are endless, as if they were specially designed to disorient visitors . . . Which is what generally happens . . . I don't feel well . . ."

"It's all so confusing . . ."

"I didn't want the money for any practical reason. I didn't need it to buy food! I have a state pension . . . and as you know, I spend very little . . ."

"Of course, Pierre."

"There were other, deeper reasons, Monsieur Rivette; it's as if I could smell something lurking nearby, very near . . . I took the money . . . just so as not to block . . . the passage . . . It sounds paranoid, but that's how it is. Unless I'm just looking for excuses!"

"I think you need to calm down, Pierre."

"Do you remember that young lady you gave my address to more than a year ago? Her husband was in the Salpêtrière. Madame Reynaud."

"Yes, yes, Madame and Monsieur Reynaud. He died, if I remember rightly. A very young man."

"Indeed. Well it was Madame Reynaud who formally requested my help in this case. The patient is the husband of one of her friends."

"I don't see the connection, Pierre."

"I think I'm in love with Madame Reynaud."

" . . . "

"You must think I'm ridiculous: a man of my age, forty-eight, hoping to court a young lady."

"You're still young, Pierre. Now if *I* were to fall in love, at over eighty, *that* would be ridiculous. Does she know?"

"Of course not."

"What are you planning to do?"

"Return the money, I suppose, or invite Madame Reynaud to dinner at some fancy restaurant. I don't know. Everything has started spinning. I think I had too much to drink and you've been too patient with me."

" . . . "

"I think Raoul's been too patient, too. It's time to go to bed."

" . . . "

"So Pleumeur-Bodou is in the International Brigade? Good for him. A just cause, adventures in a fascinating land, the ideal vacation."

"No, it seems he has joined the other side."

"The Fascists?"

"That's right."

"Well, that, my dear Monsieur Rivette, was predictable. Pleumeur-Bodou was never a democrat at heart."

"I never predicted it. But anyway, at my age, I have given up judging. I accept people as they are, whatever they do."

"You always were an overly generous master, Monsieur Rivette."

"Not at all. It would simply be an error for an old man like me to set himself up as a judge . . . But there will be judges, Pierre, you can be sure of that, judges hard as stone, who will not know the meaning of the word pity. Sometimes, between sleep and waking, I catch a glimpse of them; I see them at work, deciding. They piece it all together; they are cruel and follow rules that to us seem entirely arbitrary. In a word, they are dreadful and inscrutable. But by then, of course, I'll be gone."

"Perhaps it's because I'm drunk, but the night smells of something strange."

"Every night has a different smell, my friend; it would be unbearable otherwise. I think you should go to bed."

"But tonight's smell is special, as if something were moving in the streets, something vague and familiar, but I can't quite remember what it is."

"Go to bed. Sleep. Calm your spirit."

"The smell will follow me there too."

• • •

That night—the last hours of the seventh of April, and the early hours of the eighth—had the ambivalent honor of being one of the worst nights of my life. I can't remember what time it was when I went to bed, nor in what state I climbed the stairs. I slept, if that shivering can be counted as sleep, in a low-roofed, gray-and-white labyrinth, architecturally reminiscent of the Clinique Arago with its circular corridors; sometimes the dream-corridors were broader and stretched off endlessly, sometimes they were narrower, like twisted vestibules, and the starts and groans with which I woke and fell asleep again were not the worst of it. What was I doing there? Was I there of my own free will, or was some external force holding me in that place? Was I looking for Vallejo, or for someone else? I believe that if the company of nightmares conspired to visit me all at once, the result would be similar to what I experienced that night. I remember thinking at some point, as I sat on the bed mopping the sweat from my neck with my pajama sleeve, that the dreams I was enduring had all the features of a transmission, yes, a kind of radio transmission. And so, as if my dream-world were a crystal set secretly tuned to a private radio station, scenes and voices were transmitted to my mind (I should point out that the dreams had the following peculiarity: they were composed not so much of images as of voices, whispers and grunts), scenes quite unrelated to my own fantasies—I had simply become their fortuitous receptor. The demented radio drama assailing me was no doubt an anticipation of hell: a hell of voices connecting and disconnecting in a buzz of a static that was, I presume, my troubled snoring, forming duos, trios, quartets and entire choruses advancing blindly through an empty chamber, a kind of empty reading room, which at some point I identified as my own brain. At another moment in the dream, I also thought that the ear was the eye.

An abridged version of the nightmare might run something like this:

A first voice says: "Who the devil is Pierre Pain?"

"There is a leak."

"All I know for sure is that there is a leak."

"It could have been caused by a trivial oversight."

"Look around you, examine the view. Do you notice anything strange?"

"Our life in the Market, in the streets of the Great Market . . ."

"Dreams, melancholy."

"There is a leak, examine the view."

Indistinctly, as in a blurry photograph, I see Terzeff, Pleumeur-Bodou and myself standing around Monsieur Rivette, in the study of his old apartment on the Boulevard Richard Lenoir, where he has not lived for many years; it is 1922 and the four of us are silent, although our master's eyes are moving constantly, as if he could sense an intrusion. I understand that this image is, in some way, resisting the general drift of the dream, and that, in spite of the protection it is affording me, I will not be able to hold onto it.

A stranger smiles. He is a movie actor, but that is all I know, nothing more. His smile is beautiful, but his words lacerate the air; in a second they absorb all the oxygen in the room: "What do you mean when you say a leak? What does the word *leak* signify to you?"

From behind the stranger I think I can hear a muffled, intermittent roar, like a darkened backdrop, and it fills me with a sense of urgency.

I wake up. I listen attentively to the sound of the pipes.

Almost imperceptibly, the walls of the room appear to be vibrating. The same phenomenon is affecting my skin.

The stranger walks away along an empty boulevard. The treetops are shedding dry leaves. Is it autumn?

Now I see myself hidden behind a curtain, peering through dirty panes of glass, watching the stranger, who is standing in the middle of the street. The stranger, in turn, is examining the windows of the building in which I am hidden, though not the particular window through which I am spying on him.

Who is he? What does he want?

The scene breaks up just as his gaze is about to fall on my window.

I hear the following sentence, pronounced very poorly by two voices in unison: "It's hard for us to get around Paris, boss; we hardly know four words of French . . ."

"What does the word *leak* mean to you?"

"Leaked information?"

"Put that miniature spinal circuit away!"

"Our agents are investing energy as well as time!"

"Do you know what those words mean?"

"Time . . . Energy . . . Time . . . Energy . . ."

"A bundle of unlikely leaks."

Murmurs of boredom and disgust. Then complaints.

"Listen, boss, I have a funny feeling."

"As if my back were being scratched, as if time had already run out."

"The melancholy of dreams, their absolute futility."

"Is there anyone here, apart from us?"

I can see—as if I were down in a sewer, looking up through a drain—a man's dark shoes and his gray trousers, but only up to the knee. When he moves away a little, his lower body is visible, up to the waist. I never see his torso, much less his face.

The man is walking down an empty street, always following a real or imaginary edge. At no point does he move out of my visual field.

Someone whispers, right in my ear: "Watch out for the South American . . ."

Looking back over my shoulder, all I can see is darkness; I see that I am indeed in a sewer . . .

Blurry old photographs from 1920: Pleumeur-Bodou, Terzeff and I are crossing an iron bridge; when we reach the other side we turn and raise our hats—except for Terzeff who waves a white handkerchief—bidding farewell to a dim and gradually disappearing silhouette. I come to a square and see that a gallows has been set up; a *new* gallows, Terzeff and Pleumeur-Bodou remark, but their lips barely exhale an infrahuman sound; a mild autumnal breeze blows in through the windows, but is it autumn?

The same voice, although this time I know that it is coming from within me, insists: "Watch out for the cold South American . . ."

Cold? Cold nerves? The cold of death?

I try to say that the man is sick, that somewhere in the city there is a sick man, but although my mouth is hanging open, I cannot make any kind of sound.

"Have you heard of a nova?"

"Electrical mercury, broken thermographs, leaks . . ."

"Have you heard of a human nova?"

"All the usual quantum jokes."

"Search me."

My god, I think, looking at the shiny toes of the man's shoes, just so long as he doesn't bend down.

I wake. I am sweating, I try not to fall asleep again. For a moment I am certain that there's someone else in the room.

At the end of a hospital corridor, a woman with her back to me is laughing (I know because that is the only audible sound). Her laughter is like a sedative. Then everything falls apart and reassembles itself.

A stranger approaches surrounded by an intermittent sound. The sound is his halo. He is standing on a staircase in the Louvre. Autumn wind swirls around the Parisian skyline. He speaks to me.

"I live in the black arcades, in a patio with a glass roof."

"Suppose we have two panes of glass in contact with each other; if we look at them from the front, we will not notice anything unusual, but if we look at them side-on, we will see that there are indeed two panes . . ."

"Who the devil is Pierre Pain?"

"He kept our money."

"Is there anyone here, apart from us?"

I feel that someone is scratching at the windows. I feel I am losing my voice. I wake up.

Madame Reynaud called at my lodgings very early the next morning. It was the first time she had done so since the beginning of our friendship.

Slightly disconcerted by the novelty of the situation, I begged her to take a seat while I got dressed in the adjoining room. She didn't seem to hear me; for a few moments we stood quite still, as if observing each other from an unwonted angle, both of us held by some combination of urgency and shyness. There was not the slightest sound from outside, except perhaps the murmuring of an indecipherable presence in the air, suspended matter; and the light delineating her silhouette had the gray intimacy of certain Parisian mornings. She smiled sweetly, although with a certain reserve, and looked at everything with the curiosity of a vaguely disappointed little girl. It is true that my poor room could hardly have been untidier; in that narrow space were crammed two high-backed armchairs (family heirlooms), an old Moroccan carpet, a set of oak shelves, a chest of drawers with a gas ring on top of it, a dark table with a mahogany border on which the books I consult each day stood in somewhat haphazard piles, a microscope, a metronome, my pipes, plates and cups, a dirty knife, and so on, all adorned with a fine layer of dust, which although it had escaped my notice until then, stood out, in Madame Reynaud's presence, like irrefutable proof of squalor. I tried to excuse myself for the state of my room; I lied, saying that recently I had been too busy for housekeeping, but she put me at ease by making a conventional remark about the absent-mindedness of intellectuals. I thanked god that the door to the other room was shut. A small framed photograph hanging on the wall caught her attention; it was a picture of a street in Clichy that a friend had given me many years before. She pointed to the photo rather nervously:

"Were you born there?"

"No, no," I hastened to reply.

"It's a beautiful photograph, but very sad . . ."

"There is something melancholy about it, I admit. But I hardly notice it. It doesn't have any special significance for me. I might even have put it up to hide a damp patch."

She looked at me for a moment and then her lips relaxed into a broad smile. She was about to say something but stopped herself. Among the innumerable things she could have said, I imagined a formal, affectionate sentence, the only one I didn't want or didn't have the courage to hear. I was a coward and it has cost me dearly.

Within a few minutes she was explaining what had brought her to my apartment. It was easy enough to guess. Madame Vallejo had telephoned the previous night, to tell her about the conversation with Lemière. The outcome had been disappointing. Lemière had indeed said, "All the organs are in perfect working order," but later, alone with Madame Vallejo, he had added: "Let's hope we find one that is diseased! I can see that this man is dying, but I don't know what from."

The mention of death, more devastating perhaps coming from Lemière himself, had left Madame Vallejo in a state of almost total desperation, understandably, given the days she had spent at her husband's bedside, barely sleeping, tormented by a host of doubts; but she had reacted, Madame Reynaud told me, with an energetic resolution, and now she was requesting my presence at the hospital. It seemed, from what I was hearing, that Madame Vallejo would not rest until she had exhausted every avenue. *Every avenue* was, of course, a euphemism designating me.

Suddenly, like the waning moon peeping through a gap in the clouds, the scene appeared before me stripped of all semblances: two women determined to save a poor wretch from dying turn to another poor wretch when science and medicine have failed or refused to help. It was deeply sad, almost worthy of a late 19th-century naturalist melodrama; and yet, behind what might be called the stage or the foreground, hidden by the scenery, I thought I could glimpse—it was just a hunch, and meanwhile I remained steadily attentive to Madame Reynaud's words—the silhouette of a stranger, smoking in the wings, as it were, and I knew without a doubt that he was the South American mentioned in the dream.

I wondered if I wasn't getting carried away. What kind of purity was Madame Reynaud laying, almost unawares, at my feet? In any case, I was unworthy of it. I had done nothing to deserve it. I probably felt, as I have felt on precious few occasions, blessed.

We arranged to meet at four in the afternoon in a café near the Clinique Arago. I spent the following hours at home, alone, smoking and drinking occasional cups of tea, but I had nothing to eat. The view from my bedroom window was of attics and chimneypots gripped by a winter reluctant to be gone.

I tried to read but found the mere activity repellent. Madame Reynaud's presence was still quivering in the air of the apartment. At one point I remember throwing the book at the wall, but not in anger. I tried in vain to summon up a particularly troubling and revealing image engraved by Félicien Rops. The gray of the city outside became a black and white amalgam, harboring threats. I tried to tidy both rooms. I gave the suit I was wearing a brush. I contemplated my perfectly combed hair in the mirror. Impossible.

When I went out, clouds had covered the sky again, and before I had walked two blocks it began to rain. I hoped that the rain would last well into the night so that I would be able to fall asleep listening to the drops hammering on the roof. That was all I hoped for, and it was the best mental preparation for seeing my patient, at last.

．．．

Vallejo's room had poorly whitewashed walls on one of which hung an incongruous gold-framed mirror. We arrived to find a dark man smoking in the corridor, with the lapels of his overcoat turned up; he addressed Madame Vallejo in an incomprehensible mishmash of French and Spanish. Before she could introduce him to us, he said good-bye and left; we went into the room. Monsieur Vallejo was asleep. In a corner, sitting on a white chair, was a visitor wrapped in an outsize trench coat, distractedly leafing through a sports magazine. When he saw us, he stood up, but Madame Vallejo stilled and silenced him with a peremptory gesture:

"Best not to wake him," she whispered.

I nodded and approached the bed on tiptoe. In the mirror I could see the man returning to his chair and Madame Reynaud going to stand by a window with half-closed Venetian blinds. Madame Vallejo was the only one who didn't move.

I went straight to Vallejo's side. He turned over and opened his lips but was unable to articulate a word. Madame Reynaud raised one hand to her mouth, as if to stifle a cry. The silence in the room seemed to be full of holes.

I held my hand a foot above the head of the bed and prepared myself to wait. The patient's angular face lay before me, exposed, displaying the strange disconsolate dignity shared by all those who have been confined in hospital for some time. The rest is vague: locks of black hair, the collar of the pajama top loose around his neck, healthy skin, no sign of sweat. His hiccups were the only sound in that quiet room. I know I could never describe Vallejo's face, at least not as I saw it then, the only time we ever met; but the hiccups, the nature of the hiccups, which swallowed everything as soon as you listened carefully, that is, as soon as you *really* listened to them, was simply beyond description and yet was accessible to everyone, like a sonic ectoplasm or a Surrealist found object.

I referred to "the nature of the hiccups," and one of their peculiarities, perhaps, or so it seemed to me, was that they were self-generated. A hiccup, as we all know, is a muscular contraction, a spasm of the diaphragm producing a sudden breathing in of air followed by a closing of the glottis, resulting in a characteristic sharp sound, repeated intermittently; Vallejo's hiccups, however, seemed to be quite autonomous, foreign to his body, as if they were afflicted with him rather than the other way around. That was what I thought.

I spent two hours at his bedside. Luckily the man in the trench coat left after only a few minutes. The sound of the door closing softly behind him called me back from the speculative byways on which I had been wandering, and directed my attention to the illness, to the pit before me: my patient, Vallejo. I was delighted to discover that being with the two women and the sick man was like being alone, but alone in a harmonious buoyant solitude, swifter than clocks, as the philosopher said.

"He's awake," whispered Madame Reynaud.

I look at her and raise a finger to my lips as if to intimate: Quiet, Vallejo is asleep, he is hardly moving, his frailty is palpable. Madame Vallejo comes to the head of the bed, on the other side, opposite me. With a gesture I beg her to move away. As Madame Vallejo returns obediently to the foot of the bed, I notice that Madame Reynaud's face has suddenly turned pale. Vallejo has opened his eyes, he is looking at his wife, mumbling two or three indistinct words. He is delirious. Then he shuts his eyes and seems to be sleeping calmly. I have not moved. I feel as if a tiny but formidably heavy spider were running across the back of the hand I have been holding in the air all this time.

As I walked to the door I felt utterly drained; my shoulders ached as if I had made an inordinate physical effort, and I didn't feel like talking. I wanted to clear my throat out in the open, where I wouldn't disturb anyone, and go for a walk on my own as night began to fall. I firmly believed that my patient would recover, and in that hope I felt at one not only with the two women who had watched me from their respective corners of that room, but also, extravagantly, with most of the inhabitants of Paris, oblivious as they were to what was happening there.

Madame Vallejo's eyes were trained on me inquisitively.

"There is hope," I said dispassionately as I reached the door.

Madame Reynaud was still at the window. She looked in my direction (but she was not seeing me) then opened the Venetians.

"There is hope." I smiled, looking for some kind of sign in her bearing.

"Good-bye, Monsieur Pain," Madame Reynaud's lips seemed to whisper.

I understood that she was grateful and was going to stay with Madame Vallejo. That was all. The hiccupping had stopped; I didn't realize at the time because the sound went on echoing in my head. Naturally, I felt happy.

Before leaving I glanced at the bed-ridden man. He was dark and the sheets were white and harsh. At that moment everything seemed deceptively simple, or at least open to simple solutions. I was convinced—and not entirely without reason—that I could cure Vallejo.

"I'll come back tomorrow," I said.

The two women nodded in silence.

They were at the window, clasping each other's hands.

"At three in the afternoon," I said.

The door closed. I was alone. This is the moment when something should happen, I thought; and yet the people I passed as I walked down the clinic's dimly illuminated corridors toward the exit barely even noticed me. At the reception desk I asked the nurse on duty if she could give me the names of the Spanish doctors who were working with Lejard or Lemière. She looked at me as if I were unhinged, then went to pick up a black book, but changed her mind before opening it. The only Spanish doctor was Doctor Mariano Roca, she affirmed.

"Could you describe him?" I asked with my most charming smile.

"Old and fat," she said with disgust.

"And he's the only Spanish doctor on the staff?"

"The only *foreign* doctor," she specified. "Our medical staff is made up of French citizens, with the unfortunate exception of Doctor Roca." It was clear that the Spaniard was not in her good books.

"Are you sure that there aren't two Spanish or South American doctors who work here, from time to time perhaps, young men, about thirty years old?" I insisted.

"And what are you? A detective?"

"No, god forbid . . . Do I look like a detective? I'm just trying to return something that belongs to those two doctors."

"What?"

I examined her carefully for the first time. Her face seemed to be undergoing a gradual transformation. Now it combined the features of a guard dog and the fearfully anticipated prostitute of my adolescent fantasies.

"It's a personal matter, you understand."

"I'm afraid I don't."

"Anyway, if you're sure they don't work here . . ."

In the street I decided to take a taxi and go home immediately. The air was fresh and it was no longer raining, although the paving stones in the street were shining, as if freshly polished, and some people were still walking with their umbrellas open.

When the taxi pulled up in front of my building, I told the driver to wait, but explained that I would not be getting out.

I looked through the window of the taxi. The entrance hall was a mass of pure shadow, and there was no one to be seen, although there could well have been someone hidden in the darkness. I could feel the desire to return to my apartment evaporating.

"Switch off the motor," I said to the driver. "We're going to wait a little."

The driver turned around to look at me and nodded without saying a word, his hands resting compliantly on the steering wheel. I looked up and down both sidewalks—no sign of the Spaniards—but decided to wait. Fifteen minutes later, I told the driver to go. I watched through the back window to make sure that no one was following us.

"Are you following someone or is someone following you?" asked the driver.

I didn't answer.

What have you got to lose here? one of the Spaniards had asked.

Maybe that was the heart of the matter: losing or finding something.

"What do you two have to lose?" I replied.

The thin one blinked.

"Don't be stubborn," he said.

I suspected they hadn't understood, but it didn't matter.

"It makes no sense to me," I continued, "but it's some consolation to think that nobody could make sense of what you're trying to do. You're just giving me money."

When the thin one saw me take the envelope containing the two thousand francs and slip it into one of my jacket pockets, his blinking turned into a smile.

"You can't even imagine how little I have to lose," I said, excusing myself. "Nothing, in fact."

"Don't worry," said the dark one, smiling, "We have a lot of money, it's not an issue."

"And besides, don't underestimate the imagination."

"The imagination can imagine anything."

"*Anything*," said the thin one.

"Leave Vallejo to us, we'll take care of him; he's a friend, a dear friend."

A dear friend? The imagination can imagine anything? I had a sharpening sense that I didn't understand what they meant.

"Place Blanche." My voice gave the taxi driver a start.

"Where?" he asked, accelerating suddenly.

"Place Blanche."

The driver looked at me in the rear-view mirror, bewildered. We had gone around the block and were back in the street where I lived. For a moment I thought he was going to refuse and I felt a flutter of fear at the thought of being left alone in the street, near my apartment.

"Keep going, keep going, I'll show you the way."

I got out of the taxi in a street that was, I thought, close to the residence of a friend whom I was planning to visit and perhaps inform of my ongoing adventures. But after a while I changed my mind and instead went wandering through streets I vaguely recognized, which in the course of my walk, as the minutes went by, became gradually stranger, until I knew for certain that I had entered a completely unknown neighborhood.

I went into a café: the roof, the walls, the tables, the seats, everything was green. As if the proprietor had, in a fit of madness, tried to give it a jungle-like ambiance or, as I later thought, endeavored to camouflage the premises, and partly succeeded, although in a way that was clearly inept.

I sat at one of the tables, under a motionless two-bladed fan, which was also green, and scrutinized the interior, deserted except for two blond boys, three tables away, sitting quietly with their half-empty glasses.

"The service is a bit slow here," said one of them after a while. I didn't realize at first that he was speaking to me.

"Pardon . . ."

"I said the service is a bit slow here. The waiter has gone off to pee."

The one who had not spoken lifted his hand to his mouth and stifled a little giggle. I observed them more closely. They were very young, neither could have been more than twenty, and very carefully dressed. I told them I was in no hurry. In fact I was tired, and the tranquility of that eccentric café was doing me good.

"Sometimes it takes him half an hour to pee. It's tempting to think he's up to something else, but no, he's just trying to urinate, to squeeze out a few little mercurial drops . . ."

"Poor thing," the other one chimed in.

"It's an odd place, this," I ventured to remark.

"The Forest . . ."

"The what?"

"The Forest . . . that's what it's called."

"Most appropriate."

"The underwater forest," said my interlocutor, pointing to one end of the café.

I looked in the direction indicated by his finger and saw an enormous rectangular fish-tank backed by satin curtains.

"You can go and have a look. It's nothing special, but you're sure to find something to pique your curiosity."

I went across to the tank. On the bottom, resting on a layer of very fine sand, were miniature boats, trains and planes arranged to depict calamities, disasters simultaneously frozen in an artificial moment, over which indifferent goldfish were swimming back and forth.

I guessed that the miniatures were made of lead; their details were remarkably realistic.

"There are no bodies," I murmured, more to myself than to make conversation; nevertheless one of the boys heard, or perhaps intuited, my words.

"Look carefully."

And there, indeed, next to one of the trains, beside the last carriage, half buried in the sand, was a little man-shaped figure. It was not the only one: near a single-seater airplane, leaning against a pumice stone, another figure surveyed the almanac of calamities, a figure made of dark gray, unpainted metal, standing tall, although, had the stone been removed, it would in all likelihood have toppled irrevocably.

"Interesting."

"The light doesn't help much. A cold, white light would be ideal, rather than this Indochinese green. But the ideal, as you know . . . only by miracle . . ."

"Are you the . . . creator?"

"We are."

A world submerged and preserved, where the only flags flying were flags of death: the goldfish. But even they seemed afraid.

The shadow of a smile flickered on the boy's lips.

"It's no big deal, but it was fun finding the miniatures; you can't imagine how hard it is to find *good* lead trains . . . Look at that one, on the left there . . ."

I looked for the one he was pointing out. A splendid black train with more than ten carriages, *Meersburg Express* painted on their sides. The locomotive was blue; for a few moments I was puzzled by the black spots standing out against the sand, scattered all along beside the train. Then I realized: they were severed heads or bodies buried up to the neck. A string of corpses, but, oddly, there were none inside the train, which apart from the effects of the water had come through unharmed.

"It's German. We had to order it from Germany."

"The Meersburg Express?"

"That was Alphonse's idea. He painted the lettering."

I looked at Alphonse. He was sitting up very straight and wearing an absent expression.

"It seems the waiter does indeed have a problem," I said, walking back to my table. "Are you, by any chance, the owners?"

"Oh no," replied the one who seemed inclined to speak. "We're clients."

"It doesn't seem to be a very busy place."

The young man hesitated slightly before answering.

"Sometimes it is . . . but usually it's quiet . . . Not many people come here . . ."

"Perhaps it's an exclusive establishment, which appeals to a more artistic clientèle . . ." I suggested.

"Oh, I wouldn't say that." He tried on a smile; his teeth were extremely white. "There aren't many artists in this neighborhood, although of course that's a subjective opinion."

As before, Alphonse let slip a little giggle, which he hastened to cover up with the back of his hand.

"My brother and I are intending to move. This," he said with a vague gesture that took in everything, "is not really where we belong."

That was when I realized how extraordinarily alike the two of them were. I wondered if they might be twins.

"And where are you thinking of moving to?"

"New York. The problem, as I'm sure you'll understand, is money. We couldn't afford even half the fare. Occasionally, just occasionally, I dream that we've swum all the way there. Do you know what dreams about water mean?"

"No, I don't."

"Nor do I. But crossing the ocean in a single night is no joke. Money is always so tedious, don't you think?"

I didn't answer.

"And not many people are interested in fish-tank scenes. We manage to sell one from time to time, mainly around Christmas, but the buyers have ideas of their own and we only do underwater cemeteries. We're not prepared to compromise. Oh, the trouble we've had with clients, don't let me start . . . people are so greedy and ignorant."

"Poor things," said Alphonse. And then he murmured an unintelligible phrase of which the only word I understood was *anamnesis*.

"They order nativity scenes; it's funny, don't you think? They order battle scenes, historical reconstructions, from *us* . . ."

His face remained dispassionate. Ensconced in that chair with its green back, he seemed to be surveying his joys and sorrows with a charming detachment.

"So I suppose business is not exactly thriving."

"Your supposition is correct. No, it certainly is not. This is the only tank we've been able to place in the last few months," he said, lifting his chin with disdain or perhaps affection—I couldn't tell—to indicate the aquarium which I had already admired. "And I don't think the owner of The Forest is entirely satisfied." He smiled at his brother. "Something of a character, the Forest Ranger, wouldn't you say, Alphonse?"

"Oh, yes."

"Bladder or prostate problems, I'm not sure which, but he seems to go through agony every time he pees. He must have picked up an infection in the colonies . . . Or some such story, anyway, judging from appearances . . ."

"Why New York? Is there some particular reason?"

"Ah . . . New York." He seemed reluctant to change the subject. "I would almost say it's instinctive. There's no future here for two young men like us. We're not partial to the Surrealists or to men in uniform. And sooner or later one camp or the other is bound to throw down the gauntlet. Sooner, the way things are going."

"The sad thing is, we won't be able to leave," said Alphonse.

"Don't be defeatist," said his brother, in a scolding tone.

"Well, it's true, we won't be able to," Alphonse insisted.

"How absurd! Of course we'll leave. On an American ship. We could even mount an exhibition of miniatures in fish tanks and make ourselves a tidy sum . . . Not on the ship, of course, I mean here, in the neighborhood somewhere . . . We could achieve a certain notoriety . . ."

"But . . ."

"It could even become the fashion! Couldn't it?" he said, looking at me.

"It's not such a far-fetched idea," I conceded, "as long as the underwater cemeteries are not all the same."

"They would be *almost* the same." His eyes flashed. A formidable young man, I thought.

"But we don't have enough money to buy a single tank, or a single lead figure," complained Alphonse faintly.

"If worse comes to worst, we could ask Dad," whispered his brother.

They continued their discussion for a few moments, inaudibly, at no point losing their composure.

Suddenly, as if he had been listening to us, a waiter sprang from the shadows. He was a blond man of about my age, wearing a short lime-green jacket. His resemblance to the young artists was excruciating.

"What would you like?" he murmured uncomfortably, without looking at me.

"Mint cordial," I said.

The waiter ducked his head and disappeared. The talkative young man smiled at me: An appropriate choice in these surroundings, he said. Alphonse seemed to be on the brink of tears.

By the time the waiter placed the glass of mint cordial before me, I had reached my limit. I got up, said good-bye to the young men and went out into the street. Everything was different outside, or at least that was what I wanted to believe.

Two cars pulled up by the empty sidewalk and more than fifteen people proceeded to emerge from them, as if those automobiles had been granted an exemption from the physical laws of this world. The passengers were wearing fancy dress, and eventually, having paused at length, taking the time to survey the deserted street, chat and make apparently witty remarks, much to the amusement of their companions, they all went into a three-story house. I don't think I have ever seen people wearing more elaborate garments; yet in spite of the skill and imagination invested in those costumes, the prevailing impression they gave was one of propriety and sorrow (sorrow for a loss that is known to be definitive).

Instinctively, I stopped at a safe distance from the house and stood there, admiring them. I identified a marshal from Napoleon's army, a Roman consul and a medieval knight, who were gathered attentively and flirtatiously around a Catholic saint; they were preceded by a very old man—although his wrinkles might possibly have been part of the disguise—dressed as a Chinese mandarin, with a black costume, full of folds and flounces, on which a gold dragon was embroidered. The mandarin was, without any doubt, the leader of the cortège, and for a moment I could hear him speaking a suggestive, energetic, incomprehensible Volapük.

Two adolescent girls who had stopped beside me were observing the spectacle. Both were clasping text books and notepads and wearing expressions of rare gravity. I felt it was only polite to smile. Perhaps my change of expression was too abrupt, or caught them by surprise. I felt that our status as sole spectators implied a certain complicity. In any case, as soon as they noticed me smiling at them, they took fright and walked away, exchanging rapid and emphatic comments that I was unable to understand. I imagined the worst and for a few moments considered following them, all the way home if need be, so as to explain that by smiling I hadn't meant to suggest anything, anything at all. But I resisted that impulse. They had, no doubt, I told myself, misinterpreted my expression and intention, and now it was too late. Before walking away I realized that the Mandarin was watching me and smiling fiercely. That image, I thought, was anchored in the *real world,* come what may.

I was annoyed with myself. A wave of melancholy swept over me only to be replaced, a few steps further on, by a calm timeless serenity, immune to any shock. But the fear, I knew, was still there, intangible but stubborn. What did I fear? Not physical aggression, I was sure of that. So why couldn't I muster courage enough to go home or simply walk on without looking constantly over my shoulder, expecting to see the pair of Spaniards?

Eventually I returned to my lodgings, after wandering through outlying neighborhoods, among derelict stations, along avenues that seemed to go on forever and then abruptly end in vacant lots of a kind I would never have expected to come across in that part of Paris.

It was late when I got back, and the only person I found lurking in the darkness was Madame Grenelle. She was crying noisily.

"Madame Grenelle?"

" . . ."

"It's me, Pierre Pain. What has happened?"

"Nothing, nothing, nothing . . ."

"Then stop crying and go up to your room."

"Ah, my god, shit shit shit . . ."

Stepping closer, I noticed that she was drunk; a heavy, sickly smell of absinthe enveloped her. For some reason, I don't know why, the image of the two teenage girls disappearing into the crowd sprang from my memory like a delicate animal. But what crowd? The street had been deserted. A calm, inexorable sadness clambered onto my shoulders and clung there, like a hump or a younger but infinitely wiser brother.

"Come on now, let's go upstairs. If you stay here you'll fall ill, it's very cold."

"I'm bad, Monsieur Pain, but that doesn't mean . . ."

"Up we go."

"It's loneliness. Doesn't anyone understand? Look at my eye!"

I hesitated for a moment, the adolescent girls were walking down an empty, ideal, endless street . . . Then I struck a match. Madame Grenelle's shadow was climbing, step by step, up to the flaking wall of the landing. She had a black eye.

"What happened to you?"

" . . ."

"Let me see. You should go up to your room and rest. Your eyelid is swollen."

"It's the loneliness, Monsieur Pain."

"It looks like you've been hit."

"No . . ."

"Did someone hit you?"

"A woman. I'm a woman. I'm a human being too, aren't I? Sorry. This weather is awful, it just keeps raining. Why don't you sit down for a moment?"

I sat down on one of the steps.

"Your friend came this morning, didn't she? You must be happy. She's a very pretty girl."

"I'd rather not talk about that, Madame Grenelle, let's get you sorted out first . . . Yes, of course, I'm pleased . . ."

"I respect you, Monsieur Pain, something you never . . . Anyway . . . Would you like a shot of absinth? Sorry . . ."

Her hand appeared from some mysterious recess, gripping the neck of a bottle.

"No thanks. And I don't think you should be drinking either."

" . . ."

"I'm tired, Madame Grenelle, I've had a busy day, you've no idea how much . . ."

"Me, I'm alone all day, with nothing to do, you know, I get bored. You've never been in my apartment, I'll invite you in one day so you can see it, not a speck of dust . . . But in the end that's boring too. And it takes no time at all to clean, it's so small. My little palace."

I sighed. I felt deeply weary.

"Don't you have anything you can put on your eye?"

"Mascara . . ."

I think I smiled. Luckily she couldn't see my face. It must have been a wretched sight.

"Well, better leave it then, just rest."

"A damp handkerchief's the thing, men are so impractical."

"Excellent idea. Now stop drinking and listen to me. Go to bed."

"You must come and see my apartment one day. Not tonight. I don't think it's a good time. Some day, though, whenever you feel like it. You'll see how spick and span it is!"

"I'm sure it is."

"Help me get up . . ."

Before shutting the door of her room, she said:

"Forgive me if I've bothered you. I didn't mean to bother anyone. Do you know how I did this to myself?" She pointed at her swollen eye with the neck of the bottle, which she had been gripping firmly all this time. "I fell over while I was dancing, here, in the corridor, on my own. Ridiculous, isn't it?"

"I don't think so. Dancing is beautiful."

"You're a gentleman, Monsieur Pain. Goodnight."

"Goodnight, Madame Grenelle."

I slept well and soundly, and if I dreamed, I also had the good sense to forget my dreams. I woke late—it was becoming a habit—and having performed my ablutions went down to breakfast at Raoul's café.

While I was waiting I picked up a morning paper that someone had left open on a table, and my eyes wandered from the headlines to the filler stories and then to the photographs, unhurriedly searching for something undefined.

I must have appeared downcast, because Raoul asked, from behind the bar:

"Bad news?"

The news was about the war in Spain: the latest on the bombing raids, the shelling, and new weapons that we hadn't known in the Great War.

"The damned Germans are testing out their arsenal," said Raoul.

"Rubbish, they don't have anything special," remarked a mechanic in dark brown overalls, who was leaning on the bar, drinking his glass of wine.

"So you don't think there's anything special about dive-bombing, Robert? The Stukas!" replied Raoul, who was well versed in military technology. "Single-engine, two-seater planes, with three machine guns, and they can carry more than a thousand kilos of bombs!"

"The way you talk, it's like you're worshipping them."

"Of course not! Not at all . . . ! But you do have to admit . . ."

"All right, Raoul, I didn't really mean it, but we're not talking about the eighth wonder of the world. People are what matters, the courage of the masses."

"A war is a war," pronounced the blind boy, sitting against the wall with his white cane between his knees. "If you don't believe me, ask Monsieur Pain."

"That's right," I said, without raising my eyes from the newspaper, with its advertisements, sports news, culture and entertainment pages, gossip columns . . .

"Thank god I haven't seen one."

Some of the clients laughed.

"You're a clown, Jean-Luc, that's what you are," said Raoul.

"I'm serious," the blind boy protested, half-joking.

"It's true," I said. "You can count yourself lucky in that respect, Jean-Luc. The scenery of war is . . . Dantesque. No: miserable . . . squalid . . . The problem is that if a war broke out, blindness would only spare you from active service, not from all the other disasters that wars inevitably bring in their wake. However wretched your life is, war can make it worse, and I'm speaking for all of us, not just you."

"See, Jean-Luc?"

"All right, all right," said the blind boy. "You've convinced me."

"They're building up their armament every day," grumbled Raoul, putting my coffee on the table, "while we're just sounding off. We need to act; we need to take a firm stand, be tough . . ."

"But what are you proposing?" asked a small, bearded man with a spiky shock of hair, who until then had remained hidden at the other end of the bar. "Do you want our incompetent government to drag us into in an arms race, on top of everything else? For god's sake, my friend, there are quite enough Nazis in Europe already."

"Listen, I don't know about Nazis, but I do know that the Germans are a threat to our country, and we should stop dreaming and face up to them."

"The French bourgeoisie is a threat too," put in the mechanic, "for the French working class."

"Monsieur Pain doesn't work," said the blind boy. "Nor do I. We can't."

"How about you do us a favor and shut up, Jean-Luc?" Raoul requested patiently. "The gentlemen here are trying to have a serious discussion about the fate of our homeland."

"Ah, yes, the sweet homeland . . ." said Jean-Luc.

"Anyway, it's the poor who go to fight in the front lines, and suffer behind the lines too. Isn't that right, Monsieur Pain?"

"Officers get killed occasionally, too, Robert."

In fact I couldn't remember seeing many dead officers. The bombs, the gas, the diseases destroyed us, a terrified, stupefied troop of farmers, factory workers and deluded *petits bourgeois*. No, I don't like wars. At the age of twenty-one I had both lungs scorched at Verdun. The doctors who collected my body never understood how I managed to survive. Willpower, was my reply. As if willpower had anything to do with life, much less death. Now I know it was sheer luck. Which is no consolation. Sometimes I remember the doctors' pale faces, tinged with a monstrous but *natural* green, and their weak smiles hovering, ready to accept any kind of explanation. It's my life, I told them. Behind their faces, I remember scraps of a field hospital and, beyond, folds of grey sky, the portent of a storm.

From then on, supported by a modest invalid's pension, and perhaps as a reaction against the society that had imperturbably sent me forth to die, I gave up everything that could be considered beneficial to a young man's career, and took up the occult sciences, which is to say that I let myself sink into poverty, in a manner that was deliberate, rigorous and not altogether devoid of elegance. At some point during that phase in my life I read *An Abridged History of Animal Magnetism*, by Franz Mesmer, and, within a matter of weeks, became a mesmerist.

"Do you know what Mesmer's teacher was called?" I asked Raoul out of the blue.

"No," he said.

They were all quiet, looking at me with a certain apprehension.

"Hell . . . He was the first to try to cure illnesses by means of animal magnetism. That was his name: Hell." I laughed good-naturedly, in the stupid belief that I was immune to misfortune. "Hell was one of Mesmer's teachers, what do you make of that?"

Raoul shrugged his shoulders.

"A joke?" proposed the blind boy.

For a few moments no one said a word. A girl in a blue skirt opened the door, and a gust of cold air entered with her; it seemed to wake us all up. I remembered Madame Reynaud's face and my egoism. The girl sat on the blind boy's knees and whispered something in his ear. Hello Claudine, I heard Raoul say. I looked across at him: he was wiping glasses and nothing seemed to have disturbed the habitual tranquility of his face.

"So you're engaged in the study of mesmerism?" The question was put by the small bearded man, who had come over to my table.

I replied in the affirmative. The use of the word *engaged* seemed promising.

"I imagine you have heard of Doctor Baraduc."

"Indeed. I have read *Vital Force*."

"It's interesting," he said as he sat down beside me, "that you mentioned Hell. As an instance of synchronicity, I mean . . ."

"I don't understand."

"Excuse me. It doesn't matter. I'm not so sure I understand myself. Synchronicity, diachronicity, juggling . . . I suppose you know that Hell was a priest."

"A protestant minister."

"It's interesting that the clergy played such an important role in the investigation of animal magnetism or vital force, as it later came to be known, thanks to Baraduc, among others. And he, of course, collaborated with a priest, Father Fortin . . ."

"Best not to ask *what* he fought in." It was a bad joke but we both smiled; the bearded man was pleasant company, resolved to make the conversation enjoyable both for himself and for his interlocutor, and I felt no hostility toward him, as opposed to most of the people I had encountered over the previous days.

"Let me introduce myself. My name is Jules Sautreau."

"Pierre Pain. What were you saying about synchronicity?"

"I fear I was too hasty in my choice of words . . . Synchronicity, blotches on the wall, messages abhorrent in their sheer impossibility . . . In any case I wasn't referring to the clergymen associated with our friends."

"Do you have an interest in animal magnetism?"

"I notice that you prefer the original name. No, I'm not an adept, if that is what you mean, but in the course of my reading I have made some incursions into that field, out of idle curiosity, I hasten to add, simply for my own amusement. I'm an amateur, who takes more pleasure from the works of Edgar Allan Poe, "Mesmeric Revelation" for example, than from scientific treatises, for which of course I have all due respect. A careful search can sometimes turn up curiosities. Have you ever had occasion to read *The Human Soul: Its Movements, Its Lights and the Iconography of the Fluidic Invisible?*"

"I have consulted it from time to time."

"Fascinating, don't you think . . . *With seventy paraphotographic plates . . .*"

"But the phenomenon of the needle has been discredited, like the impression of photographic plates without contact."

"You don't think it's possible to affect them with one's own personal vibration?"

"I think it's possible to do much more than that." (I was tempted to add: by understanding mesmerism as a kind of humanism, not a science.) "In any case, what interests me is drinking from the sources."

"*De planetarum influxu,* the heavenly bodies rolling on a billiard table, all that nervous music, is that what you mean?"

"You seem to be familiar with the mesmerist bibliography."

"Only the titles," he hastened to add. "Baraduc cites some of them, and the rest, the paraphernalia, can be found in Bersot's *Mesmer, Animal Magnetism, The Turning Tables and Spirits.*"

"Yes, of course, the veils, the shabby opulence that seems to be permanently associated with mesmerism. Frivolous implements, as I'm sure you'll agree, which serve one purpose only: to disfigure and obscure . . ."

"And poltergeists."

"Poltergeists are a kind of smokescreen."

"Except that as a smokescreen they turned out to be ineffective and indeed drew the fire of the Royal Society of Medicine, which obliged Mesmer to give up his practice. Publicly, at least."

"In fact it was a way of putting hypnotism on trial, so to speak. Mesmer believed that almost every illness could be traced back to a nervous disorder. And that was unacceptable for certain individuals and pressure groups, it seems. You could say he was fighting a losing battle from the start. The Royal Society of Medicine is not known for its tolerance."

"And yet in 1831, they issued a statement that was favorable to the theory of animal magnetism."

"Yes, but Mesmer was already dead by then and his followers, as you suggested, were more interested in poltergeists than the truth. Then, in 1837, his theories were definitively condemned, and Baraduc's later experiments could do nothing to change that. The whole business is rather like a Punch and Judy show. You could see it like this: illnesses, all of them, are produced by nervous disorders. Disorders that have been engineered, coolly planned in advance, but by whom? By the patient, the environment, god or Destiny, what does it matter? . . . Hypnotism should reverse the process and bring about a cure. Should make it possible to forget, in other words. Pain and forgetting and their causes, and us caught up in the midst of it all, think about it for a moment . . ."

"A genuine utopia."

"Or a malignant illusion. When I think of those eighteenth-century doctors and healers, I can't help feeling for them. It's an idle sympathy, if you like, but sympathy all the same. I'm a utopian too, in fact, but a static utopian, unlike them. For me, mesmerism is like a medieval painting. Beautiful and useless. Timeless. Trapped."

"Trapped?"

I kept quiet for a moment, stilled to a quiet *within* quietness, gazing at the table's shining surface.

Fascination, horror, I thought, and here I am playing Doctor Templeton, but with a poorer memory.

"I don't know why I said it . . . Trapped . . . A trapped idea . . . I suppose I meant trapped in time."

"Or trapped by someone."

"By Father Hell?"

A deep-seated sense of decorum prevented us from smiling.

It was raining when I went to leave the café. A fine

rain, almost made of air, barely perceptible. I shivered with cold. Then, straight away, even before I had stepped off the threshold, I heard the howl. It sounded like the howl of a wolf. Surely it was only a dog. I froze; the street was unusually empty; I thought perhaps it was a horn that someone had sounded, a visitor to one of the buildings looming around me. A solitary, unsettled music. A foreign music (from the North Pole, I thought, or Africa), a music with its nerves on edge. I looked back through the glass door into the café. Sautreau was sitting at the same table, idly perusing the newspaper that I had leafed through. The pages touched the tip of his beard as he turned them over. Raoul, visible down to the waist behind the bar, seemed to be listening intently to the girl, whose arms were raised as if she were asking to be lifted to her feet. The others were talking, probably about the war in Spain or cycling, but I couldn't catch even a syllable. I buttoned my coat up to the neck. After a few eternal-seeming seconds, I heard the howl again. The musician's intention (since it was a musician, I was no longer in any doubt about that) was easy enough to construe. A cavernous yet lacerated sound, collapsing out of the vaults above and reverberating off the closed windows of the houses. A sound that swept the empty streets for a fraction of a second. Like a horn. But it wasn't a horn. A huge and futile pity possessed me. I froze.

• • •

At five to three in the afternoon, I reached the Clinique Arago. The rules of the institution stipulate that, before passing through the double doors that lead into the depths of the building, visitors must leave their name and the name of the patient they have come to visit, or at least the patient's room number. Having satisfied this requirement and begun to walk away, I heard the nurse's voice calling me to a halt.

"You can't go in," I was informed.

At first I thought that I had heard incorrectly or that there had been a misunderstanding, so I gave my name again and that of Monsieur Vallejo, adding that I had already visited him the previous day and was returning in compliance with a specific request from his wife. I stressed the specific request. The nurse seemed to hesitate for a moment and then looked at me curiously. She took a manila form from a drawer and read it twice; then she put it straight back into the same drawer, gently shaking her head.

"No one is allowed to see Monsieur Vallejo," she said, lying. "Those are the orders."

"But they are expecting me."

"Come back another day," she suggested, rather uncertainly.

"Madame Vallejo specifically asked me to come. She must be in the room now, with her husband. Tell her that I'm here. I can't leave without seeing her. Please . . . I beg you to make an exception."

The nurse wavered for a moment, moved perhaps by my appeal. But she soon reaffirmed her ruling.

"It's impossible, those are the doctor's orders," she said, as if they had been handed down from God.

"Which doctor?"

"I don't know, it doesn't say here, but orders of this kind can only be given by a doctor, as I'm sure you understand."

I raised my hands in exasperation.

"Will you let me see the form?"

A weasel-like smile came over her face and I understood that she was not going to let me pass.

"I'm afraid not, it's against the rules, the orders are confidential, but if you think I'm lying . . ."

I weighed up the possibility of walking down that corridor with or without authorization, but the absurdity of the situation, and sheer surprise, held me there at the reception counter with the force of a magnet. I tried another approach:

"May I send for Madame Vallejo? I will wait for her here."

"I already told you. It's out of my hands, there's nothing to be done." Her face was growing pale, taking on a milky quality, as if to match her uniform.

I insisted.

For a moment I was prey to the deluded belief that I had convinced her. She asked me to wait, opened a camouflaged door in the wall behind her, which I had not noticed until then, and vanished so quickly I could only glimpse a rectangle of reddish darkness, as if the adjoining space were a photographer's darkroom. When she came out, she was accompanied by a tall aide with blond hair and the melancholy jaw of a boxer.

The nurse now seemed to have taken on the role she'd been waiting to play all her life.

"Show this gentleman to the door," she ordered.

I was dumbfounded.

The aide came out from behind the counter, moved smoothly to where I was standing, and told me, in a harsh Brittany accent, to be reasonable and follow him.

With all the resolve I could muster, I tried to ignore him. I think I failed.

"What's going on?" I managed to sputter.

Sitting at her desk, the nurse was leafing through the bulky visitors' register.

"Calm down," she said, without looking at me.

Then she lifted her eyes from the tome and hissed:

"Go on, get out, and don't you ever set foot in here again."

After the first minutes of bewilderment, which I spent walking around a few neighboring blocks, unable to make up my mind to depart but not feeling brave enough to face a new skirmish with the nurse, I decided to hole up in a café, from which I could keep watch over the clinic's main gate.

My intention was to stay there until Madame Vallejo came out, and then explain it all to her. At six in the evening my hopes began to fade. At eight I was still there, held in place by inertia more than anything: had Madame Vallejo finally appeared, which by then seemed unlikely, I would probably not have been able to recognize her, since it was completely dark.

At nine I decided to leave and call Madame Reynaud. With a frown of irritation, I discovered that I did not have her number with me. I would have to go home, find my notebook, and go out again to call her.

I stopped a taxi. I had already grasped the door handle when I felt a blow on my back, almost a casual shove. The man responsible had a stitched-up eyebrow, not entirely covered by a sticking plaster.

"I saw it first," he said. He seemed to be speaking with his mouth full of water.

I looked at the driver to see if he would adjudicate, but he simply shrugged his shoulders. We had to resolve the dilemma ourselves. The man with the split eyebrow was waiting. I ignored the blow and assured him in the most polite manner that he was mistaken: he could not have seen the taxi before I did, because, for a start, he was not even in the vicinity when it pulled up.

He did not answer me.

"However, be my guest," I added.

By way of a reply, he reached out with both hands, gripped the lapels of my coat and lifted me off the ground.

"Mouthy Jew," he said, thoughtfully. "I saw it first."

Then, having apparently changed his mind, he let me drop and got calmly into the taxi.

"Wait," I shouted, as I lay on the ground.

I didn't feel humiliation or rage or any of the emotions that are normally provoked by an incident of this nature. I felt an irrational desire to make him stay and talk to me, to scrutinize his glowering face, to ask him where he came from, what he did, whether he had ever been inside the Clinique Arago, even as a visitor, whether he *knew* something, anything that could qualify as a certitude. Suddenly I felt more tired and alone than ever.

Then I got up as best I could, stirred by belated indignation, with the unavowed aim of returning the blow. I opened the back door of the taxi before it pulled away and managed to glimpse my attacker's impassive mug, in profile, just as the tire rolled unhurriedly over my foot.

"Shit!" I cried, embarrassed, as the taxi drove away down the street.

With one knee on the ground, I felt my toes through the shoe leather, trying, absurdly, to make the gesture look casual. Then I tried walking; it didn't hurt.

At ten-thirty, in a café full of smoke and serious drinkers, I found a telephone from which to call Madame Reynaud. I should have guessed that nobody would answer, but I kept trying every fifteen minutes, without any success, until one in the morning.

Clearly Madame Reynaud was not going to return home that night. It was also clear that she had to sleep somewhere. Where? With whom? The question was painful, not to mention futile, and made me feel ludicrous and pitiful, in the eyes of my casual drinking partners as well as in my own. I don't remember how it started, but between phone calls I had fallen into conversation with three young men determined to finish the night as drunk as lords. They worked at a printer's and were talking about women and politics. We're philosophizing, they declared. I couldn't say why they accepted my presence at their table—or did I invite them to sit at mine?—since I hardly opened my mouth, and when I did it was only to reply with monosyllables to their stock remarks about love and women, sports, and crooks both great and small; and yet, when the café closed, staying with them seemed the natural thing to do.

I don't know how much time we spent together, or how many places we went to. I remember a woman's face, a redhead, she was crying in a dance hall, an old guy in a dinner suit with a smile full of new teeth, the roof of a bar made of wooden laths, cats and trash cans, the shadow of a child or a monkey, fragments of sentences about fascism and the war, and a hand-written sign that read:

Lulu
Unavoidable
Solitude
Horns
Sex
True

"Horns? Bull's horns! But that's Spain!" said one of the boys.

"Lulu gets them all horny," said his companion, yawning.

At some point—we were all fairly drunk—someone suggested we try our luck at a dubious gaming house. I vaguely remember an alley, I think it was in Montmartre, although I couldn't swear to it, and a series of doors promptly opened by someone who remained hidden. I considered asking the time, checking my wallet, and leaving, but I didn't. Suddenly I found myself sitting with my back to a circle of gamblers in a stuffy, malodorous room, barely illuminated by a flickering light globe hanging from the ceiling. I heard shouts and cries; I made no attempt to find out what they were playing. I went back the way I had come and the same shadow opened the doors for me. Before reaching the last one, I stopped. My guide, I noticed then, was holding a cigarette. The glowing cigarette end and the buttons of his doorman's jacket shone like unreachable stars.

"Can you tell me your name?"

"Me?" replied a high-pitched voice; the shadow trembled.

"Yes."

"Mohammed . . ."

"Tell me, Mohammed, what are they doing now in that room?" I pointed roughly in the direction of the place I had just left.

"They're playing a game," he said, sounding relieved, as if he were talking to a child. "They're playing The Lady and the Butchers. Pornography."

"Pornography?"

"Why didn't you stay? I've never seen the whole show, I always have something to do. Opening the door, shutting the door, letting the gentlemen in, showing them out. But I think they disembowel a chicken. And they take photographs of the lady . . . A very effective atmosphere, I assure you . . . She is naked and surrounded by small dead animals . . . I'm the one who cleans it all up in the morning . . . With soap and water . . ."

I had seen nothing of the sort. I had a premonition. I told him to wait and retraced my steps. When I opened the door of the room, all I could see was a poorly illuminated stage on which a black man was tapping at the keys of an old piano with one finger. The tables were unoccupied—as if the clients or players had suddenly vanished, leaving a chaos of plates and glasses—except for one, in the middle of the room, where various men and a girl who can't have been more than twenty were huddled, following the fortunes of a card game. Among them I recognized one of the printers, his hair a mess and his eyes open very wide, as if an invisible hand were strangling him. I shut the door without making a sound. Mohammed was behind me. I gave a start.

"Are you afraid of something, Monsieur? If I can assist you in any way . . ."

"Afraid of something? What do you mean?"

The Arab's teeth shone in the darkness.

"I don't know . . . The world is full of threats . . ."

"Threats, yes, but not dangers," I said.

"Excuse me, my mistake . . ."

"Show me the way out."

"But Monsieur, you went to the wrong door, the show is not in there . . ."

"It doesn't matter, I'm leaving."

"This way, Monsieur, you won't regret it . . . It's subtle, very delicate, the Lady of the Chickens will make you scream inside . . ."

"I said I'm going."

He looked at me and smiled again. I noticed that he was ill.

"The Lady is well worth seeing . . . A man of the world like yourself . . . You'll be able to appreciate . . ."

I didn't reply. A bell rang somewhere. The Arab raised his nose and sniffed something in the passage. He seemed to wake up.

"All right. Follow me," he said. Now his expression was mean and bitter.

We went back through an endless succession of doors. I heard the muffled cries of what I supposed were excited clients, applauding something that I could only vaguely imagine. Walking beside me, the Arab was once again an obliging, faceless shadow. When we arrived at the last door, I handed him some coins. He hastily spat out a few words of thanks and shut the door behind me. Then I realized that I was not in an alley but a kind of industrial warehouse, an enormous, antiquated edifice, with a large gap in the roof through which the stars were visible.

I retreated, feeling my way back through the darkness, but was unable to find the door again. Where the devil had I ended up? I had no idea.

The warehouse seemed to be frozen in a moment of its own destruction. When I struck a match, the only thing it illuminated clearly was my own hand, too pale and definite for my liking. There was something in the air, something that didn't bode well. I took a few wary steps, testing the lie of the land. There had to be an exit somewhere.

The match went out and I lit another. At the back of the warehouse, I could make out an iron machine that resembled a windmill, about nine feet high and equipped with improbable blades; around it reared other metal contraptions, rusted and immoveable. It was clearly a warehouse full of useless junk, but at first I couldn't determine the nature of the objects or the uses they might once have had. Peering around, I thought I could recognize a number of household items, although they were completely deformed by the passage of time. Gradually my steps became less hesitant. In spite of the general neglect, there was some kind of order to the way the junk was piled, and it was possible to move along narrow aisles between rows of old camping stoves and metal ironing boards, big bronze vases and rotting wooden chests. After a while I discovered that all the passages led to the centre, where the objects were not piled high but scattered haphazardly, leaving a large space from which, with better lighting, one would have been able to survey the rest of the warehouse.

I shouted.

Unsurprisingly, my shout was absorbed by the towering piles of junk, like a stone dropping into the void, without producing the slightest echo. If I had been hoping that a hypothetical guard or night watchman would respond to my call, I gave up on the idea straight away. I resigned myself to looking for a sheltered place in which to spend the rest of the night. Near the windmill that presided over that singular cemetery I found a kind of bathtub or vat and, after lining the inside with sacks, I tested it out and found that it was not altogether uncomfortable. In any case, I guessed that it would not be long till dawn.

Before falling asleep I lit two more matches; a few yards from my makeshift bed I noticed farm tools: dark shovels covered with a crust of tarry earth, sickles, pickaxes, pitchforks, blue and gold harnesses, oil lamps with broken glass bulbs, axes, and a collection of pokers of various sizes leaning against a board in perfect order. The implements of an ideal farmer.

I know I had begun to fall asleep, because I had already discerned certain faces that recur in my dreams (or perhaps it would be more accurate to say *the weight* of those faces) when the sound woke me up. A drip of water, that was all, but right in the center of my consciousness. I opened my eyes; I wasn't afraid; I waited.

The noise repeated itself, an imperfect duplicate, coming from somewhere between the rows of dark masses in front of me and to the right, as if it were being made by something creeping along against the wall. Careful not to make the slightest sound, I felt in my pockets for the matchbox, extracted a match and held it between my fingers, without lighting it, like a weapon or a talisman, waiting for my curiosity to ferment.

I should say that if I was still afraid, my fear (though the term is hardly exact) was swallowed at that point by the fatalistic calm that resulted from knowing without a doubt what was producing the sound and from the resigned decision not to make any attempt to find out why. One thing at least was clear: the sound was moving intermittently in my direction. I thought: Now it is following the wall, but in a while it is bound to veer toward the center, toward me. It would probably turn when it drew level with my position, but it might also continue on its way so as to approach from behind—in fact, it was bound to do that.

I admit that for a moment I did weaken; unable to bear the situation any longer, I wanted to strike the match, to illuminate the scene that I sensed was being set up around me. The darkness was so sheer, the drip was moving at such a regular pace, the bath was becoming so cold and was so reminiscent of a coffin, that an act of any kind would have sufficed to fracture the desolate coherence, the twisted lucidity distilled by that sound and the warehouse. Yet I made no movement.

I feared that cramp would seize my legs if I remained in that position much longer. I could feel a burning at the base of my esophagus. My eyes were aching.

Suddenly the noise moved away from the wall and began to thread its way through the junk. Which meant that its source would appear on my right. With the back of my neck resting against the curved edge of the bath and my legs drawn up, I leaned sideways as far as I could, staring in that direction. Curiously, all my senses were sharpened not by fear or the imminence of combat or revelation, but in a more artistic way by the perfectly de-limited space in which the anticipated silhouette would soon materialize.

The steps slowed down, skirted a piece of furniture, a wardrobe, perhaps; I heard a rustle of clothing, then silence.

I intuited a tremulous presence in the darkness. I knew that I was being observed. I counted to three, then tried to strike the match only to find that my fingers were no longer holding it. I tried to get up; my arms slipped on the sides of the bath without making a sound. Huddled in the bottom of the tub, like an archetypical victim, I tried to take out another match. The box was in one of my coat pockets, but at first I couldn't find it. Finally, I held my meager torch aloft and looked out: I couldn't see anyone.

Whoever it was had stopped about ten yards from the bathtub, out of my field of vision.

Although I could not see him, I could hear his hiccups. The sound was perfectly clear. Spasmodic and irritating.

"Vallejo?" I stammered, in a voice that failed even as it emerged from my lips.

There was no reply.

The shadow hiccupped again, and I understood, as if I had put my head into a whirlpool, that the sound was not natural but simulated: someone was imitating Vallejo's hiccups. But why? To frighten me? To warn me? To make fun of me? Or simply moved by some unfathomable sense of humor and disgrace?

Come on, I thought, keep coming.

I don't know how long I waited.

After a while I realized that he would not take another step.

Little by little, the stillness, which had been tense at first, lapsed into ordinariness.

Twice I tried to get up, and slipped both times, as if my destiny were forbidding me to run the slightest risk. The light began to change in the sector of sky visible through the gap in the roof; soon it would be dawn. At some point, perhaps while making my final attempt to get out of the bath, I uttered *Uh* or *Ah*, my sole protest, more a cry of desperation than a bid for help.

• • •

I woke with stiff limbs, an unrelenting ache in my neck, and a frightful hangover. It was eleven in the morning and a glassy dust was falling, or rising, through the gap in the roof. The warehouse was quiet; the junk was stubbornly guarded by an aura of neglect: objects banished from the realm of human concern—even the light seemed to shun them. It was not hard to find the door; it had no handle and opened onto a gravel-strewn courtyard with abandoned flowerbeds on either side. The morning, the sky's crown, seemed to be falling apart. Which was comforting, in a sense, since I was in a similar condition. To the left I noticed a metal door, which was shut. Beside it was a little wooden box, which seemed to have been waiting there for centuries; I sat down on it. I took a deep breath. Images of the previous hours—escape and disappointment, dreams and delirium—tumbled through me. It's finished, I thought aloud, the carriages bound for nowhere are finished. The sky over Paris, though clearer than the day before, seemed more sinister than ever. Like a mirror hanging over the hole, I thought. But we could never know for sure. An indecipherable tongue. I urinated against a wall, profusely. I was tired; I felt wretched, alone, and confused in the midst of a labyrinth that was far too big for me. I didn't know what to do. I couldn't tell whether the sky was shaking or I was.

Before long I was out in the street, looking for a taxi that would take me to the Boulevard de Courcelles.

Conscious of my unkempt appearance, rumpled clothing, and bristly face, I rang the bell. While waiting I smoothed down my hair again. The toes of my right foot were hurting; maybe the taxi had cracked a bone and I was just beginning to feel it, maybe it was the result of my cramped position in the bath.

The door opened slowly, without a sound, and from within (the curtains must have been drawn) there emerged the hooked nose and then the deathly pale face of a woman who must have been about seventy. Either she had slept as badly as I had or she had recently been crying. She looked at me bewildered, murmured something that sounded like an excuse, and gently shut the door. I rang the bell again.

The old woman reappeared almost immediately:

"Madame Reynaud is not here. I'm Madame Reynaud senior. Who are you?"

She had blue eyes and her voice was unsteady. She must have been beautiful many years ago. Now she only seemed afraid.

"My name is Pierre Pain, I am a friend of Madame Reynaud's." Madame Reynaud junior, I thought, and almost burst into hysterical laughter. "It's extremely important that I see her."

My words made her smile almost imperceptibly and perhaps feel nostalgic for the world, with its gallantry and boating.

"Well, it won't be possible for a week."

I must have reacted with an alarming grimace, because the old woman stepped back in fright.

"She has gone to Lille, to her aunt's house," she exclaimed from the darkness of the entrance hall.

Then, remaining in the dark, she added in a murmur, as if to ensure that I was fully informed:

"I am her late husband's mother."

• • •

At one in the afternoon I returned to my lodgings. I filled a basin with water and washed my head and torso, briskly rubbing my forearms, armpits, neck and chest until they were red. Then I changed my clothes and went out again. Something, a sense of solidarity more than a premonition, was telling me that there was no time to lose.

I returned to the Boulevard de Courcelles, to Madame Reynaud's apartment. The old lady seemed more animated and listened with philosophical resignation to the puerile excuse I had invented. No, Madame Reynaud junior had not left that day, but the previous night. Her mother-in-law could not confirm (or deny) that she had been nervous, since she had, as usual, seemed rather *distant*. Although she's young, you have to understand that she's a widow, already well acquainted with misfortune, Madame Reynaud senior informed me from the threshold, with the door just slightly ajar. Her daughter-in-law had packed her bag in haste shortly after receiving a telegram from Lille. Yes, she took the telegram with her. A raised eyebrow: had I been intending to pry into private correspondence?

The conversation lasted no more than a few seconds. I went to the public telephone in the first café I could find and dialed Madame Reynaud's number. There was no answer. While drinking a glass of wine, I reflected that there were two possibilities: either the old lady was in the habit of not answering the telephone, or Madame Reynaud had given me a different number. For some reason I found myself accepting the second hypothesis unreservedly (opening it, in other words, to the wildest conjectures). There was no telephone in Madame Reynaud's apartment, therefore the number she had given me and which I had called on numerous occasions, reaching Madame Reynaud herself each time, didn't belong to her telephone. And yet she called it "my home number." For anyone else this problem would have been a triviality, or at most a kind of riddle, but for me it was like a nail hammered into my patience, and the problem was compounded by the singular and unexpected journey my friend had undertaken, a journey that seemed unthinkable, given her concern for the health of Madame Vallejo's husband, but also because she had not left even a brief message to inform me of her departure.

Still disturbed by the events of the previous hours, I called Monsieur Rivette from the same telephone. I don't know why. I was acting on a blind impulse. I felt a kind of indistinct anger, a vague resentment at having been fooled, which was gradually hardening me from within like a carcass being stuffed by a taxidermist.

"It's Pierre Pain; this business is getting complicated."

" . . ."

"I don't know what to do . . . I'm losing my grip . . . my grip on reality . . ."

" . . ."

"I don't even know why I called . . . What's to stop me breaking off this friendship . . . It's a hangover from what turned out to be a complete waste of time, although we really knew that even then, didn't we? . . . A few nights ago I dreamed of you . . . You looked very old, as old as you are now, in fact . . . Wrinkled and worried . . . But in the dream it was 1922, and the others were there, you know who I mean . . . Why am I thinking of them? . . . They're like ghosts . . ."

" . . ."

"You were looking all around, but only your eyes were moving, as if you had a nervous tic, or were being very slowly strangled . . . It wasn't exactly reassuring . . . Were you looking for someone hidden in the room? . . . Or a message, a few undeniable words . . . I don't know . . . This morning, yes, I had an awful morning, I thought we all had to die . . . You, me, and everyone we might in some sense call a fellow traveler . . . The sorcerer's apprentices . . . As a joke it's pitiful, but that's not the point . . . The only hiding place was in the roof . . . Was it a spider? . . . You knew we were being watched from the corners of the room . . . I realized and was frightened . . ."

" . . . "

"As if someone hidden in the ceiling had pointed me out . . . Why me? . . ."

" . . . "

"I'm not exaggerating, dreams don't exaggerate, I'm desperate . . . Not because I think that something extraordinary is happening, but because I feel I'm losing everything . . ."

" . . . "

"What? Not much, almost nothing, but I didn't realize before . . ."

" . . . "

"Excuse me for calling . . . I'm better now . . ."

" . . . "

"Sympathy? . . . I feel for you as one man on death row might feel for another . . . Look at us, look where we've ended up after all these years . . . It's pathetic . . . Here I am insulting you on the telephone . . . Forgive me . . . I think Vallejo . . . my patient . . . is going to be assassinated . . . Don't ask me how I know . . . I don't have any rational explanation . . ."

" . . . "

"All of us are implicated in this hell . . ."

" . . . "

"Good-bye, you never did me any harm . . . or any good, either . . ."

"   . . ."

"   . . ."

I hung up. The rude way in which I had ended our friendship came as a complete surprise to me as well as to Monsieur Rivette. And yet I felt better, lighter, cleaner. To be honest, after hanging up I had to make an effort to contain my laughter.

Poor, venerable Monsieur Rivette, none of it was his fault, but nor was he the elder with immaculate hands, living in neutral territory. In fact, I thought with wicked satisfaction, old Rivette deserved a good dressing-down. I lingered over the expression: *dressing-down*. In some bizarre way, the disaster lay hidden behind it. Then I understood that the old man and myself were alike not only in our attitudes towards the labyrinth, but also because we were both spectators.

Absorbed in my own problems once again, but in a better mood already, more inclined to reflection, and free of anger and resentment, which obscure everything, I went to dine, as I did from time to time, in a restaurant which, although reasonably priced, was reputed for its excellent cuisine.

All I could do was formulate a series of questions. What was Madame Reynaud doing in Lille? Was her presence there related in some way to Vallejo? What threats or promises could the telegram have contained to precipitate such an abrupt departure? How could I describe, or understand, my experience in the warehouse? Had it been an hallucination due to my own nervous instability, or some kind of inscrutable apparition. Was the imitated hiccupping a parody or a premonition? I had claimed that there was a plot to assassinate Vallejo; did I really believe that? I raised the napkin to my lips and closed my eyes. Yes, I did.

Lost in these and other ruminations, I spent longer

than usual over my meal. Suddenly I saw one of the Spanish men outside, the thin one, walking breezily along the opposite sidewalk. My heart almost jumped out of my chest. I couldn't believe my eyes. I left some bills on the table and ran out.

I began to follow him, at a distance of about thirty yards, initially. The Spaniard was walking with his hands in his pockets, at a relatively unhurried pace, as if he were out for a stroll and taking an interest in his surroundings, although conscious that he did not have much time to spare. All I wanted was for him not to turn around and see me, as I would not have known what to say, and for the walk not to last too long, since I could feel my strength beginning to ebb.

After a few minutes my enthusiasm evaporated. I remember being observed with interest by passers-by; in spite of the cold, my face was covered with perspiration. Smoke briefly encircled the Spaniard's neck, like a pitiless comment on my fatigue.

I soon realized that the thin man was not going anywhere in particular. He was walking energetically, true, but that was his natural way of walking. All he was doing, in fact, was strolling about, gazing at store windows and the façades of buildings, never turning to look back, as if a single glance were enough for him to record all he saw in a precise and definite manner. I wondered if it might not be best to catch up and accost him. I guessed that it would not be long, depending on the duration of his walk, before I had no choice but to do so.

Suddenly I was engulfed by the hubbub of the Boulevard Haussman and could not remember how we had ended up there. Again I saw or intuited the circular corridors of the Clinique Arago and the angular face of Doctor

Lejard projected into empty space. Although I was confused, my spirits rallied.

I could tell that the Spaniard was slowing his pace. For no reason at all, as we entered Rue de Provence, I assumed that he was heading toward the synagogue, where he would stop, and there would be someone waiting for him inside, but oblivious to that itinerary, the Spaniard continued uphill to the Place D'Orves and came to a halt on the edge of the sidewalk, pensively observing the traffic and the opening of the first umbrellas.

I took refuge in an entranceway while keeping an eye on him. There, in a tiny cubicle, a clockmaker had set up his workshop. The tick-tock of the clocks mingled with that of the rain. The clockmaker looked at me and lowered his eyes. He was old and his face was covered with tears. The weather could not have been worse; the rain was intensifying, and above the fossilized buildings, which were enveloped in a murmur that struck me, paradoxically, as similar to a nursery rhyme, a leaden sky reared, with milky patches molded by the shifty wind into lung-like shapes, forms that seemed able to breathe in and out, suspended over our heads. That was when the Spaniard looked in my direction without seeing me and lit another cigarette, sheltering the flame with his hands and the brim of his hat, before setting off again toward Rue de Châteaudun.

From that moment on the situation began to veer toward farce. For a start, the pedestrian traffic in the streets had thinned out considerably, and the Spaniard could quite easily have caught me on his tail. Even the dimmest observer would have twigged, seeing one man walking through the rain followed by another, adjusting his pace. Had there been any doubt, both of us were soaked through, and no one in their right mind walks in the rain for that long. Soon the distance had narrowed to no more than ten yards. The Spaniard lit another cigarette, and turned to look back quite openly, as if to check whether I was still there.

I stopped in the middle of the sidewalk, wet and defenseless, a perfect target for his shrewd gaze. Thunder rumbled in the distance. The Spaniard looked curious. What does he want, I wondered. For me to follow him? That much was clear. I felt despondent. The other option was to cry out. Was he the madman, or was I? Shivers ran right through my body; I was undoubtedly falling ill, and yet my mind and spirit remained alert, curious, open to—how can I put it?—to the strange confessions whispered along those unreal streets. And yet I didn't want to stay out in the rain, which shows that I still hadn't set aside certain misgivings. A steaming hot coffee and a glass of something strong would have done me a world of good.

The Spaniard smiled. We went up Rue Rodier to Rue Rochechouard. The rain became sleet, falling slantwise and slowly like a silk handkerchief. Now we were walking toward Place Blanche. I thought of Madame Reynaud; papier mâché; a plummeting fall through claws; the taxi driver who didn't know where Place Blanche was; Madame Grenelle descending the staircase. The sum of my destinies. I laughed. I knew that the Spaniard, five yards ahead of me, was laughing too. In spite of appearances to the contrary, he must be a very clever man, I thought.

Before reaching Place Blanche, we went downhill again, along Rue Pigalle, to Rue La Bruyère. We were walking in circles. When we reached Rue D'Amsterdam, the Spaniard quickened his pace again, and for a moment I thought he would get away from me. The sensible thing to do was to turn toward the Gare Saint-Lazare, and that was what I did. Before long I spotted him standing still in front of the signboard for a tiny movie theater that I had never noticed before. Having carefully inspected the poster for the film, he surprised me by proceeding to buy a ticket and disappearing into the theater. I considered the situation, which had taken an unexpected turn; I had to act decisively. The movie was called *Actualité* and was described rather vaguely as a story of love and science; the lead roles were played by actors unknown to me, a man and woman, both young, with perfect, serious faces. I had the impression they were mannequins, although they were just the standard young lovers who could have starred in any melodrama. A character actor also appeared in some of the photographs, with his face screwed up in a grimace of incredible pain and shock; the production company had made sure to point out on the poster that this was the actor's last role: "Featuring the late, fondly remembered Monsieur M . . ." M . . . yes, I remembered him, a supporting actor, with a talent for comedy, who never had much success. I suspected that his wince in the photographs owed more to the illness that finally killed him than to the requirements of the script.

I approached the ticket window.

"The movie has just begun," murmured the vendor without looking at me; she was a rather plump redhead, more or less my age, who was busy writing something in what appeared to be an ordinary school exercise book, except that its pages were pink. Verses! A poet!

I bought a ticket and went in.

An aisle divided the rows of seats, from which the heads of the viewers protruded like nocturnal flowers; they were sparsely scattered, unclassifiable, mostly alone and isolated in their places, while the images projected on the screen showed something that I mistook, at first glance, for a procession, but which turned out to be the inauguration of a palace, a ball, or some similar gala occasion.

An usher appeared on the left, the beam of his flashlight quivering on the carpet. I handed him a few coins from my pocket, then, before he could walk away, I took hold of his arm and forced him to stay. He offered barely any resistance. His muscles were like wire under the cloth of his jacket; I could feel him trembling like an animal, and guessed that his face, which I couldn't see, was sensuous and worn.

"Calm down," I whispered. "I want to sit right here. Far from the screen. My nerves are not the best."

I had meant to say my optic nerve, but it was too late to make amends.

The usher switched off his flashlight and looked anxiously at the curtains hiding the door.

"All right, don't worry, there's a free seat here, behind you, all you have to do is turn around and sit down."

"Ah, that's perfect."

"At your service, Monsieur."

I let go of him and settled into the seat. I was in the last row on the right-hand side; behind me there was only a little wooden balustrade with decorative carved pillars rising above it and the curtains that covered the back wall of the cinema from one side to the other. On the screen, the sun was coming out.

The scene was a beach, presumably in summer, a beach that was empty except for a few seagulls walking nonchalantly by the water's edge. The sand was black and shining; the sky, by contrast, was a slick of steady, unvarying light, quietly spreading over the rest of the screen. "After Paris and its parties, the sea and the beaches of Normandy were the ideal balm for Michel," recited a woman off camera, in a somewhat ecclesiastical tone, like an aging secretary who has seen it all, while at the far end of the beach a couple appeared: two dark spots, barely visible at first, taking forever to reach the foreground. The Spaniard was sitting on the left, near the aisle, about ten rows in front of me. Well, I didn't lose him, I thought, and sighed, but now came the hard part, overcoming my indecisiveness, thinking of specific questions to ask if I took the plunge—I couldn't put it off much longer—and went to sit beside him. "Michel, however, had not forgotten the whirlwind of Paris": this sentence is emphatically articulated by a different voice, the lively, capricious voice of a blonde woman, who closes her eyes with an air that is at once resigned and cross. In the next sequence it is Michel who is closing his eyes (Michel is the lead actor whose photo appears on the posters) and the following scenes have a swirling quality, which suggests that he is dreaming. First the staircase of a palace; then a motor car stopped in the Bois de Boulogne; a view over a racetrack at night; feet walking down a corridor; an unmade canopy bed, from which the sheets have been violently ripped; the face of an old man, perhaps Michel's valet, watching something, terrified; the echo of a distant explosion; the back of a man who is slumped, sobbing, over the steering wheel of a car stopped on a country road; the feet in the corridor again, suddenly breaking into a run; burnt remains of a hobo's camp on the bank of a river; and a group of elegantly dressed young people milling enthusiastically around a slightly older man, no doubt their leader, who turns out, of course, to be Michel. Imperturbably, he raises a hand to ask for silence and readies himself to propose a toast.

That was when I realized that someone was sitting next to the Spaniard.

A hitch. I don't think there could have been more than twenty people in the theater, so it didn't seem likely that the Spaniard would have chosen to sit right there, when there were so many free seats. In fact the cinema was almost empty; apart from me, there was no one in my row, and in the Spaniard's, only him and his unexpected companion: a powerful bare neck, bulky shoulders, the right ear like a scrap of crumpled parchment stuck to his temple, where some tufts of dark hair still clung. "We have to get married, it can't go on like this," says a woman's voice. Somebody puts on a record. The music is barely audible, drowned out by a mechanical squeaking, which is followed by an explosion.

Michel is sprawled in an armchair, in a dimly lit corner of the room, offering no comment. After a while, he gets up and goes to the window. Only then do I understand that he is alone in the library and that the window looks out over a cliff. It is night and the camera pans gradually down from Michel's preoccupied face to his shoes. He taps on the floor with the toes of his shoes and then there is only the sound of the waves. Impatience is going to kill us all, I thought.

The usher reappeared, followed by a hesitant client. "My life, my career, all my worldly goods are in your hands," Michel confesses, in profile, examining something off camera. A blonde woman is watching him intently in the background. The usher cleared his throat as he passed me on his way back up the aisle, as if trying to alert me to something out of the ordinary. The blonde woman raises her hands to her face. There was no reason to anticipate danger, and yet I turned around; the usher was behind me, half hidden by the curtains, which gave him the air of a Roman patrician, timeless and indifferent to the turmoil and seductions of the screen. "We'll get married, of course," says Michel with a melancholy smile, "but we shall have to accept the verdict of fate." I turned back to the screen: again there was only the endless beach under the snow-colored sky, and the two indistinct figures coming toward the viewers. I stood up. The usher had disappeared and all that remained where his shadow had been was a slight fluttering of the curtains. With my first steps I realized just how wet my clothes still were. I hesitated. "The main obstacle to loving you is my memory," says Michel. "During the day, amnesia is like a desert. At night, it is like a jungle, inhabited by wild beasts. Do you still believe that we could find happiness?" The woman's face stands out against a background of grassy dunes. A maddening sun pulsates over the sea. While the screen was shedding so much light, I made my way to the Spaniard's row. Then it all went dark and I sat down promptly, embarrassed by the sound of my wet clothes.

It is night, and Michel and Pauline (the blonde girl, whom he has married) are at Michel's home in Paris. The servants are observing them in silence. Michel's valet (a youthful version of the old man who, in previous scenes, saw something that we can only assume was terrifying) is making an effort to please his new mistress. "Who is the cook?" asks the girl. "I am," the valet replies. There is something defiant in his tone. All the other servants look down, ill at ease and perhaps afraid. "But if Madame would like a cook," the valet adds, "I know a woman who is clean and capable." "All right," says Pauline, without clearly indicating what she has decided, while looking at the enormous tapestries hanging on the walls of the salon.

The following scene takes place in the dimly lit library: Michel and a slightly older friend, perhaps his doctor or his lawyer, are drinking cognac and smoking, but not in a leisurely way; they are tense. In a halting voice, Michel is recounting the details of an unfortunate incident. The sound of a distant explosion. Michel closes his eyes.

The Spaniard looked at me as if he had never seen me before. He elbowed his companion to alert him to my presence. The companion was slow to react; he was totally absorbed in the scenes unfolding on the screen. When he finally turned his face to me, he simply said:

"Hello, Pain, how are you?"

I was at a loss to reply. The years had certainly left their mark, and yet I recognized him instantly.

"Life is sweet and you're still young, my friend; pull yourself together." "Every night is a torment for me, Paul." "Be brave." "You can be brave when you know what you're fighting, but I don't. My enemies are in the air. No, it's worse: they're hidden beneath. They're crawling through the territory of guilt." "But you mustn't let your nightmares destroy you, Michel; remember that most nightmares have no substance." "My nightmare is the past or memory, and I would have to be somebody else to forget."

I was dumbfounded. It was Pleumeur-Bodou. He was smiling, satisfied with the impression he had made.

"You? Here?"

The Spaniard looked at me curiously, then he turned to look at Pleumeur-Bodou, as if entirely absorbed in observing our reactions.

"It's been ages since we saw each other, hasn't it? But time can't erase the memory of a true friend's mug . . . eh?"

I nodded. I was lost for words.

Pleumeur-Bodou observed me with a mixture of delight and arrogance. He was going to continue, but then he changed his mind and addressed himself to the Spaniard:

"José María, why don't you let me have your seat, so I

won't have to sit in this awkward position—you're wedged in between us there—and my friend and I can talk like normal people, without having to inform everyone else in the theater of our affairs. With a little tact and simple good manners we're sure to be well treated, even in hell . . . eh?"

After taking a moment to translate Pleumeur-Bodou's speech, the Spaniard stood up. But Pleumeur-Bodou was too fat, and trying to change seats simultaneously, they got in each other's way. For a moment they were stuck. Someone behind us complained. From another seat came an irritated Shhh. The theater might have been small and old, but its clients were serious movie-goers. Pleumeur-Bodou sat down again.

"Look, José María, you get up first and sit down here," he tapped the leather upholstery of the seat to his left, "and when I have moved here," he touched the Spaniard's chest with the tip of his index finger, "then, but only then, you can take my seat."

"What are you doing here?" I muttered. "How do you know this man?"

He winked at me.

"Just a moment, Pain, be patient."

José María had stood up again, but one of Pleumeur-Bodou's paws forced him back down into his seat. The Spaniard smelt of wet clothing. I looked at the screen: Michel was sleeping on a couch in the library. In the foreground his wife and his friend (who was also his doctor) were observing him and speaking in hushed tones, as if they were afraid of disturbing his sleep. A tragic aura envelops the whole scene. "He was top of his class," says the friend. Pauline is crying. "One of the country's rising stars; he had everything . . . he lost everything . . ." Watch carefully now, said Pleumeur-Bodou. The images that appear on the screen, like a dramatization of Michel's nightmare or an illustration of the doctor's story, have a different texture, composition and photographic quality, which suggests that they come from another film: a group of young scientists appear before the camera in various situations, first in a spacious laboratory, then strolling through a park. Look carefully, Pain, whispered Pleumeur-Bodou, his voice charged with emotion, one of them is Terzeff.

"Terzeff," I said.

Voices from the rows behind told us again to be quiet.

"Shut up, you imbeciles!" said Pleumeur-Bodou.

Terzeff and the young scientists, among whom Michel was not to be seen, flitted about the laboratory, peering into one another's test tubes, raising the flasks and joyfully proposing toasts, as if they were kids in an elementary chemistry class and the teacher had stepped out of the room. Pleumeur-Bodou stood up, he must have been at least six feet tall, and scanned the shadows for the person who had reprimanded him. He sat down again almost immediately and whispered, his face a foot away from mine:

"How do you like that? There he is! Our dear friend Terzeff, moving, laughing, younger and more sprightly than either of us! Doesn't it make you a little jealous? That's what I call the mystery of art! I mean, he's alive, isn't he?" Stoically, the Spaniard endured Pleumeur-Bodou's flesh spilling over into his seat.

On the screen the scientists had left the laboratory and they were now posing in the garden, seated on a bench, then around a fountain, and on a staircase, cracking jokes and looking boldly at the camera.

"I don't understand. What's Terzeff doing there?"

"That was the first laboratory he worked in. It was extremely difficult to get a place; there were hundreds of applicants, and against all the odds Terzeff was one of the few selected. I applied, yes I did, myself no less, and damn it, they rejected me. What do you think of that?"

"I don't know. What I'm wondering is how all that was turned into a film. You must admit, Monsieur" (I refused to adopt the familiar tone he was using with me), "that it is extraordinary to find Terzeff and his colleagues appearing in the middle of this dreadful melodrama."

"You can't deny it's a marvelous document."

"That depends on your point of view." On the screen now night is falling over the buildings of the research institute. A succession of progressively darkening images precedes the end of Michel's dream: the iron entrance gate decorated with an unreadable sign; enigmatic shadows stealing through a desolate courtyard in which the French flag is flapping; a night watchman walking across the yard with a bunch of keys hanging from his hip; the closed windows of the laboratories; the heavy metal door to the basement; a cat looking at the camera from its vantage point on top of a hedge.

"Actually, Pain, it's two different films. That fool" (he was referring to Michel) "is supposed to have studied in a scientific research institute. Now, listen to what the doctor says to his wife."

"They're all dead." Michel's friend looks at Pauline as if the confession had torn something inside him. "And yet many questions were left unanswered." Pauline's silhouette, her delicate, inquisitive profile trembles next to a huge oil painting in which the naked bodies of angels and demons are tangled.

"Who?"

"Listen!"

"That's enough, be quiet, damn you." The protest

came from three rows back and the voice in which it had been issued seemed genuinely cross.

"All of them?" "Yes, all of them, except for Michel, who was indisposed and unable to attend." "But how? What kind of accident could have . . . ?" "An explosion, an explosion that was caused by something in Michel's laboratory." "My god!" "Twenty rising stars, twenty of the nation's best young scientists, wiped out just like that." "But what was Michel working on?" "I don't know. Nobody knows. His notes were destroyed in the explosion and he has always refused to talk about it; all I can say is that it was related to radioactivity." "Then he gave up his career and the nightmares began; now I understand." "You are the only one who can help him, my dear."

The doctor takes Pauline's hand while she looks into his eyes as if he were her captor and she were in his thrall.

"That moron's wife is cheating on him with his best friend."

"Are you going to be quiet or not?"

Pleumeur-Bodou stood up menacingly.

"Why don't you just clear off, boy?" Pleumeur-Bodou rested his clenched paws on his hips, looking like Mussolini in the newsreels.

The Spaniard had turned around and was quietly looking at the boy sitting behind us, no doubt a movie buff or a student with time on his hands, or both. Somehow the boy sensed that it would be better not to pursue the dispute, and slumped down in his seat. Even seated, the Spaniard seemed far more dangerous than Pleumeur-Bodou's precariously balanced mass of humanity.

"There's always some ass-wipe."

"I had no idea that Terzeff had been an actor," I said, just to change the subject. I was convinced that the rest of the people in the theater were watching our peculiar three-man show with as much interest as the film.

"He wasn't. The director of *Actualité*—an amusing title, don't you think?—worked in that research institute in the twenties and shot a sort of promotional documentary, but it was never shown. Years later he incorporated some of the footage into the dream sequences of his feature."

"When was this movie made?"

"*Actualité*? Four years ago, at least that was when I first saw it. The scenes with Terzeff were shot in 1923, before sound; you can tell, can't you?"

I had to calm down, recover my composure, step back, escape from the sensation of unreality that was infiltrating everything. I thought: an innocent man is caught up in this. I thought: the South American is going to pay for *everyone*.

On the screen, Michel says a fond farewell to his parents. A motorcar drives into the forest. "Life is not all that important." An audience of old men is quietly watching Michel. He rubs his eyes, more and more vigorously. The gesture is a throwback to infancy. He drinks a glass of water. There are pronounced rings around his eyes. Pauline is sleeping alone in the canopied bed. "No one can blame me, no one else knows, and I am innocent." The doctor boards a train leaving Paris. Michel's valet watches the dusk through an oblong attic window. In the clean and tidy room behind him, an old photo of a footman hangs on the wall, presumably his father or a close relative, since the physical resemblance is striking, but whereas the valet has a look of melancholic resignation not without a certain charm, his father's face betrays a pure and simple terror. A man's hands break a breadstick. Bolts of lightning flash from the clouds in the far distance. Slumped in an armchair in the library, Michel covers his eyes.

"I was speaking with Monsieur Rivette not long ago; he said you were living in Spain."

"Ah, dear old Rivette, a very fine mind, without a doubt . . . Spain is beautiful, yes, and it's only the beginning . . . But Paris is my true love . . . Look now, what did I tell you, that miserable doctor is trying to steal the twit's wife."

"I need to talk with you. Let's go outside."

"I believe my presence is no longer necessary," said the Spaniard.

"All right, José María, we'll see each other later on." It was evident from Pleumeur-Bodou's tone that he was accustomed to giving orders, and yet in the way he addressed the Spaniard there was also a certain respect, a deference bordering on trepidation, of which he was probably not aware himself.

The Spaniard hopped nimbly over my knees and reached the aisle in a matter of seconds. He was thin and his clothes seemed to hang loosely about him. He did not say good-bye.

"I've only been in Paris for two days," explained Pleumeur-Bodou. "You might say I came specially to see this film. I don't know if you remember that Terzeff was my best friend."

"Yes, I also remember that he hanged himself. As it happens, a few nights ago Monsieur Rivette was kind enough to refresh my memory." The screen shows a dark backstreet; a tramp is sleeping among trash cans; there are cats on top of the cans; the street, in fact, is infested with cats of all shapes and sizes.

Pauline and a mysterious-looking stranger appear in the foreground. "I need to talk to you," says the man. "What do you want? Who are you?" "You have to trust me. For your own good." Pauline tries to flee, but the man does not let her. For a moment their faces almost touch.

"I am a police detective, we have good reason to suspect that your husband planned the explosion that killed all the staff at the research institute." "You're out of your mind, that was an accident." "We have evidence to suggest that it was a premeditated mass murder." Pauline tries to look sarcastic. "You have no idea what Michel was like after the accident." "How was he? You tell me." "A psychological wreck; he completely lost his taste for life. The memory of that nightmare was with him every moment of the day."

"Well, well, so you've been talking with Monsieur Rivette . . . I should visit the old fellow before I leave."

The detective smiles: "Perhaps he's pretending . . ."

A kind of white wave, a wave made of irresistible light, sweeps over Pauline's astonished face.

"What a sneaky devil! He's trying to get off with her, the son of a bitch!"

"Incidentally, he told me about Terzeff and Irène Curie."

"He's a wise old man, very wise, but don't go thinking he knows everything."

When they say good-bye, the detective holds onto Pauline's hand for longer than normal. Pauline looks down. Michel appears on the rooftop terrace of his house, armed with a pair of binoculars, and scans the horizon, where dark clouds are massing. Beside him stands an artifact that resembles nothing so much as an Aztec sacrificial stone. Behind him, his valet is waiting, stiffly posed.

"He didn't even know Irène. All sorts of things were said at the time; there was a lot of exaggeration."

"Let's go for a walk or find a café, anywhere. I want to talk with you. Please, I have no time to lose."

"All right. I've already seen the part that interested me anyway. I'll come back again tomorrow."

Outside it was raining.

We went into a bar on Rue D'Amsterdam; Pleumeur-Bodou ordered a rum punch and I ordered a mint cordial. We must have seemed an odd pair, because we immediately attracted the attention of the few clients, who turned, somewhat indiscreetly, to look at us. Or perhaps it was Pleumeur-Bodou's loud and peremptory manner.

"So, what did you want to talk about?"

"Terzeff, and your Spanish friend."

He glanced scornfully at my tie and lit a cigarette with a resigned gesture.

"I don't see the connection, but fire away."

I told him everything I knew about the Spaniard, from the encounter on the stairs outside my apartment and then at the Clinique Arago to the extraordinary bribe at the Café Victor.

"Well," said Pleumeur-Bodou mockingly, "you had a perfect opportunity to return the money, and you didn't."

I tried to object. I could feel myself blushing.

"Do you know why he wanted to keep me away from Vallejo?"

"Frankly, Pierre, I have no idea."

"But he's your friend, and I dare say you know the other Spaniard too."

"Indeed. But that, in itself, means little. I have many Spanish friends; I am deeply attached to some of them, others are simply companions with whom I share certain of life's pleasures. José María falls into the second category. Incidentally I should inform you that he is the great-nephew of one of our major poets, Heredia, as well as possessing a considerable income and a generous soul. But there's no more to it than that. Don't let coincidences fool you. Do you remember what Bergson said about chance? Do you?"

"No."

"He was talking about criminal chance, chance as the ultimate killer, or something like that, what does it matter, to hell with Bergson . . . You were following him and you found me. So? All the better. You'd be surprised to know how many people I run into every day. And in much stranger places than a banal movie theater. As to the bribe, my guess is that the whole thing was a joke. José María found out, from your patient's wife herself, I presume, or from some friend of hers, that you would be called upon to treat the man. Perhaps there was a bet involved—Spaniards love betting—or perhaps it was just a joke at your expense. You must remember that José María is a doctor, and so belongs to an enlightened sector of the Spanish population, which prides itself on a positivism that we find incomprehensible. Besides, as you know, wealthy foreigners are often somewhat extravagant, especially if, as in this case, they have an artistic temperament. Really, Pierre, I'm amazed that you can't tell the difference between a joke, though it was a little heavy-handed, I admit, and a serious genuine threat. I think you let your nerves get the better of you, my dear friend. Here speaks a man, I remind you, who was at the front just a few days ago."

"Yes," I murmured absently, "I heard that you had become a fascist."

Pleumeur-Bodou smiled contentedly. He ordered another rum punch at the top of his voice. His vigor and conviviality disgusted me. Even his thirst was repulsive.

"Of course, Monsieur Rivette, he's your source, I presume . . . Well, yes," he seemed to remember something important, "things are coming along."

We remained silent. Time flowed around us as if we weren't there; the other clients smoked and drank, disparate sounds drifted in from the street, the waiter wiped glasses, chunks of wood crackled in the fireplace; behind the bar someone slammed a door violently. Or perhaps it was the wind.

I thought that if I kept still I might escape from illusion and discern the presence I could sense nearby, sending me signals from an untouchable space.

"I'm going to tell you what happened to Terzeff. And this really is an interesting story. Think of it as a way of honoring our former friendship. The friendship that once bound the three of us. And by the way, there's no need to call me *Monsieur*."

"There was never any friendship between us. It was simply that, for a time, you and Terzeff were visiting Monsieur Rivette and so was I."

"All right, all right, but we were at least on first-name terms back then, weren't we?" Looking injured, he ordered another rum punch.

"What are you going to tell me? The story of Terzeff's suicide? His thwarted love for Irène Joliot-Curie? Frankly I can't imagine that luminary of French science going by the name of Irène Terzeff-Curie, or our friend helping her to discover artificial radioactivity, much less winning a Nobel prize. We must be getting old and losing our perspective!"

"You're speaking for yourself there. Now listen. The first part is wrong. Terzeff never even knew Irène Joliot-Curie, an ugly creature if ever there was one. Nor did he try to refute her mother's theories, as some claimed at the time. The real story is entirely different, and I'm the only one who knows it. As Monsieur Rivette will have told you, and if he didn't, you have since found out, Terzeff joined Madame Curie's circle in 1920. He wasn't yet twenty-three years old: one of the youngest, and clearly the brightest. At the end of 1924, for no apparent reason, he broke away and gave up the research he had been doing in that group. He would never explain what had moved him to throw away his career, or a part of it. And shortly afterwards he committed suicide. His acquaintances (as for friends, true friends, he had only one, and that was me) were puzzled by the absence of an obvious motive for his disappearance. The only way they could make sense of it was to presume that he had argued and fallen out with Madame Curie herself, a plausible enough explanation, given Terzeff's willful, independent, impassioned character; he must have tried, they said, to challenge some of the eminent lady's theoretical postulates. Nothing could have been further from the truth, since apart from the fact that it would have been difficult for a young researcher like Terzeff even to approach such an authority, he showed little interest in the work Madame Curie was doing at the time. His attention was focused on the other side of the marital bed, so to speak. He was interested in Pierre Curie and his last project. Do you know how Pierre Curie died?

"No . . ."

"He was run over by a carriage. On the 19th of April 1906, in the morning, as he crossed Rue Dauphine. At the time he and another scientist by the name of D'Arsonval were investigating the psychic forces manifested in mediumistic trances. The project was left unfinished, and shelved. It was never mentioned again; setting aside the circumstances, it was rather unorthodox, and bore no relation to Curie's earlier work. Or perhaps it did, but that only made it more preposterous. His partner D'Arsonval vanished like a puff of smoke, never to be heard of again. After the absurd accident that cost Curie his life, D'Arsonval disappeared, just like that. Perhaps that was what piqued our friend's curiosity. You have to bear in mind that at the time, like us, Terzeff was an enthusiastic if not entirely convinced mesmerist, and it must have struck him as significant that Curie was working, as it were, on the medium's plane. I don't know what Terzeff got up to, but after digging around here and there for a number of years, from 1920 to 1924, he came to the conclusion—brace yourself now—that Curie had been assassinated. I was the only person to whom he confided his suspicions, which were in any case unsupported by any firm documentary evidence, and now you are the second person to be informed of them. He always refused to reveal his reasons for making such a claim. If I told you, he said to me one night, you'd think I'd gone crazy. On another occasion he insinuated that he was keeping quiet to protect me. But to protect me from what? From madness, or what he took to be madness, I suppose. All I could piece together was that Curie had not been killed because of his research, although in a sense the work he had been doing was a good pretext for eliminating him; no, his death fulfilled some ritual function, don't ask me how. I do also recall, however, that for Terzeff every death had a ritual function; death, indeed, was the only genuine rite left in the world."

"And why did Terzeff commit suicide?"

"That was never clear."

"It's crazy. Everything you have told me is crazy. If it happened the way you say, why not suppose that Terzeff was assassinated too?"

"I don't know. Terzeff was my friend, possibly the only friend I've ever had, and when he confided in me, a few months before his death, I believed him. Perhaps it was an act of faith. But what seems to me beyond doubt is that, whether or not Curie was assassinated, my friend must have discovered something terrible that led to his own destruction."

I looked around: the café had emptied and the cold was creeping in among the tables and the chairs, the dirty glasses and the cigarette butts crushed on the floor.

"Something terrible . . . in the papers, in the notes . . . something everyone had overlooked . . . Except for Terzeff of course, with his clinical eye . . ."

Pleumeur-Bodou was gazing off into a nightmare from 1924. His expression was bloated and abject, as if he had glimpsed a light in the depths of the nightmare and was afraid.

"How does the film end?" I asked.

He looked at me in surprise.

"The film . . . " I said. "*Actualité* . . . you've seen it before, haven't you?"

"Countless times."

"How does it end?"

With a sad smile Pleumeur-Bodou said:

"Crudely. Michel kills his parents. Then he tries to kill his wife. He fails. He commits suicide. But first he sets fire to the mansion: a magnificent blaze, total destruction . . ."

"And the valet?"

"Ah, yes, the valet, that nosy smartass, he dies in the fire, and whether or not it's an accident is never clear. Or perhaps he ups and runs. Yes, that's it, he gets away. He disappears. He is swallowed by the night. It's quite a strange film . . . I don't know what to think of it. To be honest, I don't entirely understand it."

"But you've seen it so many times."

"Yes, but there are sequences, fragments, that I still don't understand. And maybe I never will, but what does it matter . . ."

"What will you do now? Will you go back to Spain?"

"Possibly. I have a number of political commitments to

attend to." He seemed to wake up. "And what about you? How is life treating you? Still as much of a loner as ever?"

I considered insulting him, but it wasn't worth the effort. Pleumeur-Bodou had spoken the truth, I sensed, although it was a truth composed of shadows on the wall of a cave. Terzeff's version would have been different. April and the circle expanding to the point of nausea. Geometry, everything was geometry and shit. I stood up.

"Are you going?" he asked in a plaintive-sounding voice.

"Yes, thanks for everything."

"What will you do?"

"I don't think I really have a choice . . . I don't know . . . We'll see . . ."

When Pleumeur-Bodou smiled, I saw the line of his lips sum up all my useless, fruitless years. I felt that unless I did something straight away, I would collapse right there, at the feet of my onetime fellow-student.

"I hope you won't be running any unnecessary risks when you return to Spain," I said, feigning concern.

"I doubt it. The Republic is doomed. No need to worry, in any case, I work behind the lines. I'm an Intelligence Officer, did I tell you? I apply my knowledge of mesmerism to the interrogation of prisoners and spies." He burst out laughing. "It's extremely effective, I assure you."

Nakedness at last, and misery.

Suddenly I felt well again. No, not well, just a little better. I felt unburdened. I realized that I was going to face something infinitely more dangerous than Pleumeur-Bodou, and that, in the end, none of this mattered much at all. I picked up his glass of rum punch and threw it in his face.

"What?!" He looked more surprised than indignant.

But after an instant of inaction, he leaped to his feet

and picked up a chair, with a clearly hostile intention. I took a step back.

"Sit down," I said. "Let's not turn this parting into a hooligans' brawl."

"I'm going to break your back."

"I have a gun in my pocket," I lied. "Come any closer and I'll fire."

"Fire then, you dog."

The barman and two clients were watching us from the bar.

"Call the police!" I shouted. In apparent response, one of the clients ran out the door.

"You're a child, Pierre, go on, get out."

He took out a handkerchief and began to dab at his face.

"I feel sorry for you," he said, without looking at me. "You're as old as I am and you don't even know what side you're on. You should kneel down and kiss my hands. Poor fool. You have a gun, do you? You? How ridiculous! Just get the hell out of here! What are you standing there staring at me for? I feel sorry for you, I really do, I really do, you're pitiful, you really are, you really are, I feel sorry for you . . ."

I left. The rain was still falling on the streets.

At seven in the evening I ordered a coffee in a café near the Clinique Arago. I was prepared to wait for Madame Vallejo to come out, or, failing that, to hatch some kind of plot to get in.

At seven-thirty, while students at a nearby table were talking excitedly and all at once about the Spanish Civil War (one was arguing that instead of sitting around chattering in Paris they should go and join the ambulance corps in Spain), I decided that I had no choice but to slip into the hospital however I could.

I paid and went out into the street, with my head down, my shoulders hunched, and the sketchy beginnings of a plan.

Hidden behind a tree, I waited for the propitious moment; I must admit that the prospect of another confrontation with the receptionist and the aide from Brittany did not appeal to me.

After a while the students who had been talking in the bar came out and headed toward the clinic. I joined them discreetly, and by the time we reached the opposite sidewalk I had worked my way to a safe position in the middle of the group and taken the arm of a student, perhaps the one who wanted to go to Spain.

"Fine ideas, young man," I said. "Fine ideas. Fascism must be stopped."

He looked at me somewhat surprised; then he smiled—almost all his teeth were decaying—and said:

"I'm afraid you're mistaken, sir. My vocation is obstetrics."

"No matter, my friend," I said. "We all have to help however we can."

He was a pleasant lively boy, and seemed very sure of himself.

We burst into the lobby noisily, as if into a dance hall. Within a few seconds I had managed to scurry away down a corridor. Young voices echoed behind me, fading away:

"Good-bye, Hélène."

"Good-bye, Paul."
"Good-bye, Lisa."
"Good-bye, Robert."

Like a deserter, like the deserter I might have been if the gas hadn't got me first, I disappeared into the hospital, frequently changing my course, avoiding the nurses and the tearful or smiling visitors who kept suddenly emerging from doors located in the most unexpected crannies.

As a result of this strategy for passing unnoticed, within a few minutes I was lost. To make things worse, there were no signs to guide visitors and the rooms were not numbered consecutively, which made it extremely difficult to orient oneself; similarly, the combined effect of the erratic stairways, each unlike the others but all burdened with superfluous landings, and the circular and semi-circular corridors, was such that even the canniest visitor would sooner or later have been unable to say what floor he was on. And my predicament was exacerbated by a determination not to ask any questions.

Soon there was no one to ask. The corridor in which I had ended up was dark and damp, with unplastered cement walls and a room on either side: a half-finished bathroom and an unlit storeroom in which mattresses and bundles of moth-eaten blankets were piled. The corridor was sealed at its far end by a wall which bore an illegible but no doubt pornographic inscription framed by a large heart, scrawled when the cement was still wet. The whole place smelled of urine, or rot, of human and animal feces mingled, as if the entire floor were coated with a thin hard crust of filth.

I decided I would take refuge in the bathroom until nine and then set off in search of Vallejo.

When I emerged, there was considerably less activity. The visitors had left, and the white corridors went past like the pages of a book written in a foreign language, barely animated by the sound of peaceful distant voices, the clinking of trolleys distributing medications or collecting the patients' dinner plates, the gurgling of tanks, and the faint rumble of the water heaters.

I only encountered two other people; the first was a nurse, who greeted me with a nod, thinking I was someone else or mistaking me for a doctor; the second was an old man inching his way along a side corridor, who didn't even look at me.

I went down and up stairs. I remember staring in fascination at a three-story house across the street as if it were a chimerical planet; I tried to avoid what I thought were the busier corridors, and, when I had no choice, spent as little time in them as possible, just enough to orient myself; I opened doors, saw the weary face of a fat man, sleeping with his bedside lamp left on; an old woman with her head sunken in a pillow and a contented expression on her face, while a somewhat younger man, her son perhaps or her lover, slept beside her in an armchair; I saw the round face of a little girl who looked back at me without fear or surprise.

The galleries stretched on and on as the minutes went by. I felt increasingly cold; my steps seemed to resonate through all the wings. I knew I would never find Vallejo's room.

It was then, as I was trying to find my way out of a section of the building in which my search had proved fruitless, that I saw it at the end of the corridor, as if it had been there waiting for me all along. It was barely more than a blurred silhouette, an armless body, a nightmare catapulted straight from infancy. It was more pitiful than frightening, but its presence was unbearable. Embrace it, I told myself, but did not entertain that thought for long. My hands were trembling. I sensed that the silhouette was trembling too. I turned and ran.

The labyrinth, the fascination of the labyrinth possessed me: each new hallway that appeared as I walked in a daze along those unevenly illuminated galleries, each stairway and elevator baited my febrile hesitation. I realized I was dripping with sweat; I leaned against a door; it opened.

There were two beds in the room, both empty. I shut the door and let my eyes grow accustomed to the dimness. The shimmering silence of a snowy landscape reigned once more in the corridor outside. I lay down on one of the beds. Branches protruded into the space framed by the window, as in a Japanese print. I thought of Madame Reynaud, the threadlike simplicity of life, the necessity of seeing her. It was cold; it occurred to me that there must have been a heater somewhere in the room. Approaching the window, I looked down and saw three people in a cement rectangle that was meant to be an interior courtyard. A lamp threw shadows that stretched to the columns of a grey arcade and beyond.

There were two men and a woman; they were talking; every now and then the woman stamped her heel; she was wearing a black skirt and jacket and carrying a handbag and a gray trench coat hung over one arm. One of the men was wearing a doctor's white coat, and the other, who was short and fat, had his hat pulled down to his ears. The man in the hat looked as if he were listening skeptically, impatiently, while keeping a wary sidelong eye on his own shadow stretching away to the base of the columns.

I would not be able to say exactly what it was that caught my attention, but having walked around the room in search of the heater, which I knew I would not find—and even if I had, my apprehensive circumspection would have prevented me from switching it on—I rushed to the window, as if I were suffocating, and pressed my nose and mouth to the glass, misting it with my breath.

I was just in time to see the fat man cross the courtyard and disappear down a corridor in which I could dimly make out enormous black earthenware tubs. The woman and the other man were still standing there expectantly, the man's face tilted forward, as if he were examining the hem of his companion's skirt, while she let her gaze wander idly over the opaque windows to her right. At one point the man produced a pack of cigarettes and held it out to her. She shook her head, barely intimating thanks, and turned her face to the left, looking doubtful, as if she were counting the windows on the other side of the courtyard now, in one of which, had she sharpened her gaze, she might have noticed my silhouette, and taken fright, seeing me there, watching them, frightened myself, exposed. Suddenly the fat man who had gone away reappeared, and the other two turned to watch him approach.

I could see well enough to notice his resemblance to Lemière (the man who had stayed resembled Lejard, but the woman was not, of course, Madame Vallejo). He waddled hurriedly over the cement, like a nervous duck. He had come straight from the arcade and seemed anxious to return to the others. The woman placed her hand delicately on his shoulder and let it linger there and the fat man (it wasn't Lemière) moved his head without looking at her, in a way that puzzled me at first. The doctor took the woman's hands; the fat man took off his hat, waited for the others to finish consoling each other, and then moved his head again. It was a simple no, a horizontal shake: right, left, right . . . Then, with an inner stiffening that gave the gesture an added poignancy, the fat man's chin fell and struck his collarbone like a bell's clapper, as if the denial had utterly drained him of freedom. The woman took her hand from the doctor's grasp and lifted it to her eyes, but then it slid down to her cheek of its own accord, like a spider, the fingers spread over her mouth. The fat man shrugged his shoulders. The doctor bobbed his head abruptly, in a falsely optimistic manner, and put his arm around the woman's waist. Offering no resistance, she let herself be led away from the arcade and disappeared directly beneath my observation post (the doctor had a perfectly round bald spot and the woman's hair had a soft look, falling in waves that glowed in the lamp's yellow light). The fat man stood there for a moment in the middle of the courtyard with his chin on his chest and his hands in his pockets, then walked away, following the other two.

Before long it was clear that whatever had been played out there was not over yet. In the strip of darkness under the arcade facing me, I saw the glow of a cigarette and guessed that the smoker was sitting on the bench that ran along the wall. I think he had been there all along and I think they had known or intuited that he was nearby; the fat man, at least, must have known, must have seen him, and probably even gave him a light, fawning and fearful, his body blocking the match's flame from my view.

I tried to tell myself that the targets of my surveillance were of no interest and certainly no concern to me; I tried. Then the cigarette traced a parabolic arc through the night air and the man showed himself, entering the lighted part of the courtyard with his hands in his pockets and the un-hurried air of an insomniac out for a walk.

It was fairly obvious that he had seen me. At first he seemed to be following the others, but then he stopped and looked straight up at my window. I think he knew I was watching him, and saw my fright, and maybe my bewilderment and sadness too. In any case, there was nothing in his stance to suggest more than the mildest interest. As if he were observing a madman, I thought (two images passed through my mind like a pair of canoes: the nurse who had barred my way into the clinic, and myself in a straightjacket). Suddenly I realized that my hands were trying in vain to open the window. After the initial surprise (I had formed no such intention) I accepted the idea, and my fingers went on feeling their way around the frame. It was useless; the window had no bolt, no sash; there was no way to open it. The man was still there in the middle of the courtyard, looking at me. I rapped on the glass with my knuckles. If he heard me, he gave no sign of it. I looked for a switch, impelled by an irrational desire to light up the room and reveal myself. To confirm my presence beyond all doubt, my *attendance*, my humble but punctual spectator-ship. The light was not working either; I had ended up in the only room where everything was broken. When I went back to the window, almost groaning, the man was still there, looking up, as if I had never left that frame, as if the room, the walls, the Clinique Arago and my body were so many transparent, ineffective obstacles to his vision, which was searching the dark sky and the stars beyond.

We stared at each other for a moment longer. Then he continued unhurriedly on his way, with muffled steps, and disappeared from my view. Once he had gone I realized the magnitude of my weariness. I looked up: a glass roof, supported by an iron frame, separated the courtyard from the night outside. Without the slightest hesitation, as if something of the stranger's self-assurance had rubbed off on me, I lay down on one of the beds and fell into a deep sleep. I woke after midnight and left, taking no precautions to avoid being seen; no one stopped me or said anything.

Over the following days my life seemed to return to its normal course. Pure and simple despair alternated with depressive episodes (which may have been religious in origin, since I regarded them as inevitable, without for a moment considering suicide, and accepted the sorrow, drinking it down to the lees), setting the tone for days of renewed lucidity, calm in spite of everything.

I did not, of course, forget Vallejo, but at the same time I understood that my small part in his story was over; there was no place in his reality for me. Madame Reynaud, who had been the bridge between our worlds, was gone, and any possibility of contact had disappeared with her.

So, from the eleventh of April on, I passed the time rereading Schwob's *Imaginary Lives* and *The Children's Crusade*, which never fail to soothe my soul, and certain pages of Renard and Alain-Fournier, which made me nostalgic for a countryside in which I have never lived, but I also went wandering around the city, and visited two good friends, with the secret intention of recounting my recent adventures, although in both cases I was unable to do so, not knowing where to start and feeling that the end of the story, or what I took to be its end, was less than convincing.

On two occasions I also tried, unsuccessfully, to reach Madame Reynaud by telephone. One afternoon, perhaps the afternoon of Thursday the fourteenth, more out of melancholy than stubbornness, I sat myself down in the same café as before, opposite the Clinique Arago, and waited there for a few hours, keeping a desultory watch by the window, in case Madame Reynaud happened to appear.

The proof of the misfortune that I had begun to intuit, the confirmation of my creeping sense that I was alone, perhaps for good, was to come on the twentieth of April when by chance I ran into Madame Reynaud on Rue de Rivoli. She was accompanied by a tall handsome man holding an umbrella. Madame Reynaud introduced him as Jean Blockman, her fiancé.

Not knowing what to say—I had no umbrella, I was getting wet and wanted to be gone—I told her about the unfortunate incident with the nurse. Her face lit up as she listened. How beautiful she is, I thought, and how wretched I am. She told me that she had come back from Lille on Sunday the seventeenth, with Monsieur Blockman, who had suffered an accident, nothing serious, as it turned out— that was why she had rushed to Lille (Blockman smiled and looked at her adoringly)—and the first thing she had done on her return was to visit Madame Vallejo, who had informed her that I had not kept my appointment.

After conferring with Blockman, she remarks that what has happened to me, the whole business, is really very strange.

"I have no idea why they kept me out," I say.

Then Blockman reminds her of the time, and Madame Reynaud says, with a fleeting smile, that they are running late.

"Of course," I manage to murmur with tainted courtesy.

I don't know if she realizes what I am feeling. Monsieur Blockman holds out his hand and says he hopes to see me again, Marcelle has spoken very highly of me. Suddenly Madame Reynaud says:

"But perhaps you don't know . . ."

I tilt my head. I feel dizzy. There were so many things I would like to know about: old Madame Reynaud, for example, why she didn't answer the telephone, shadows gliding through the Paris nights, the future.

Madame Reynaud's face is glowing; rain suits her. Blockman, at her side, is happy, looking at her all the time. Then Madame Reynaud asks if I have heard that Vallejo is dead and indeed already laid to rest; she attended the burial, it was very sad, there were speeches.

"No," I say. "I had no idea."

"A very sad occasion," Blockman chimes in; he went to the cemetery too. "Aragon made a speech."

"Aragon?" I murmur.

"Yes," says Madame Reynaud. "Monsieur Vallejo was a poet."

"I had no idea. You never mentioned it to me."

"Well, he was," affirms Madame Reynaud. "He was a poet, although not at all well known, and very poor," she adds.

"Now he'll become famous," says Monsieur Blockman with a knowing smile, looking at his watch.

EPILOGUE FOR VOICES:
THE ELEPHANT TRACK

PAUL RIVETTE

Avignon, 1858–Paris, 1940

"Even before opening the door, I knew how I would find the old man, which corner of the room he would be sitting in, what his face would try to hide. I sat down in front of him and said my piece without beating around the bush. Naturally he pretended not to understand at all, he tried to make light of it; finally he stood up grumbling, his features hanging slack, as if they were about to fall away from his bones. A face destroyed by hesitation. And perhaps by cowardice and circumspection. I told him it wasn't important, it didn't matter whether he understood or was prepared to give me any practical help, and then he seemed to calm down. There was a moment when I thought: You selfish, scared old man. Then I felt alone, submerged by the great black wave, and I was glad he was there, grateful even for the company of a man who would not commit himself in any way. I never saw him again. He died the day the Germans marched into Paris. He was found when the downstairs neighbors could no longer bear the stench coming from his room."

MOHAMMED SAGRERI

Marrakech, 1910–Paris, 1945

"On the other side of the Venetian blinds, his face wore what seemed to be a fixed expression, which might be labelled: contemplation of the void."

Having worked as a doorman at the Les Archers cabaret, near the Porte de Clichy, in 1938 and 1939, he spent his subsequent years in various poorly remunerated jobs, fulfilling his duties with diligence and a certain distance, as if he were already no longer there.

"Now we see him sleeping on a camp bed, his left hand hanging out, his face buried among the blankets, legs apart like a woman in the act of giving birth. His perfectly folded new clothes are hanging over the back of a chair. The sun is pouring in through the open windows of the room."

ALPHONSE LEDUC

Paris, 1918–Paris, 1940

CHARLES LEDUC

Paris, 1918–Vancouver, 1980

"The Leduc brothers, real little snakes in the grass; if you weren't careful, before you knew it they'd be at your throat."

The inventors of the miniature fish-tank disasters were to follow diverging paths. Shortly after Guderian and Kleist's panzer divisions broke through the front, Alphonse went out into the street and put a bullet through his head. In fact, during the Phoney War, that is, from October 1939 to April 1940, he had threatened to kill himself dozens of times. Why did he not act on those threats? Perhaps because the situation was not yet sufficiently desperate to make him pull the trigger. His twin brother tried to dissuade him but knew deep down that whatever he said, Alphonse would not be deterred. In 1947, Charles Leduc was able to board a ship bound for Buenos Aires, where, as in Paris, his fish tanks were completely ignored by the public. From then on his life was one long, slow migration, with halts that sometimes lasted longer than he would have liked, toward the magnetic, icy, tranquil north. He spent his last years in Vancouver, dealing in furniture and antiquarian books.

JULES SAUTREAU

Lyons, 1895–Montpellier, 1960

From his daughter Lola's notebook: "Dad was sweet, but intelligent too, or perhaps not exactly intelligent, but you could ask him anything you liked, and he was always ready to listen, as well as knowing twice or three times as much as you did, I don't mean encyclopedic knowledge, he wasn't some kind of D'Alembert, in fact he didn't read much at all, sports magazines, that sort of thing, but what he was really good at was sensing what you liked or found interesting, for example, when my sisters and I were students, we'd be going on about Camus, and Dad would join in enthusiastically, with a telling remark, or a critical comment, or suggestions for further reading, and it wasn't till years later that I found out that he'd never read a word of Camus, what *he* really liked was having people on . . ."

JEAN BLOCKMAN

Colmar, 1908–Arras, 1940

When Jean Blockman was called up for active service in 1939, he complied reluctantly. In April 1940, all the talk in his company was about the best way to desert. No one did; they almost all surrendered. But not Blockman, who wandered around the outskirts of Arras with a few fellow soldiers, searching in vain for an escape route back to Paris. When confronted with the enemy, he was surprised to find himself fighting tenaciously and even with a certain enthusiasm. He realized he was courageous, but above all he realized he was lucky: he had come through without a single wound. Since all the officers were dead or had disappeared, he was tacitly appointed leader by the remaining men. Remembering stories he had read in his teenage years, Blockman decided that they should sleep during the day and march at night. During the first night they came across a dozen discalced Carmelites wandering in the dark. The following night, a delegation from the Arras chamber of commerce. On the third night they met with a British patrol (consisting of three exhausted men) and after a discussion in sign language about the relative merits of heading north or west, the two groups went their separate ways with a friendly good-bye, wishing each other the best of luck. The following day, while sleeping in a ditch, Blockman and his men were machine-gunned by a German patrol.

MARCELLE REYNAUD

Chateauroux, 1915–Paris, 1985

Madame Reynaud endured the war and the death of Jean Blockman with surprising fortitude. In 1944 she was employed as a secretary by the women's clothing manufacturer Dupleix and Brothers, where she met her second husband, one of the firm's designers. They were married in 1947. They did not have children. Her life, however, was full and happy. In 1955 she became a widow for the second time. There were no more husbands after that, although there were occasional lovers. Until she reached retirement age, she worked at Dupleix and Brothers, where she was highly respected and made many friends. Sometimes when she remembered her youth she burst into tears, the tears of an old woman befuddled by a stream of incomprehensible images: her first husband's face, the rain, the sun, the cafés of the Latin Quarter, Pierre Pain, a poet whose work she had never read, not a line, the lasting tender friendship of women, the gaps in any story, gaps that slowly close as years go by, narrowing, becoming less significant, not so much gaps as blanks. She died of a heart attack while reading a travel book. Her Portuguese housecleaner found her three hours later.

MAURICE FEVAL, also known as ALOYSIUS
PLEUMEUR-BODOU

Amiens, 1895–Tarragona, 1964

"A French gentleman, all the ladies in my group of friends
adored him; he was suave, and he had a truly outrageous accent, which was the principal source of his charm, although
to be frank, it's odd that he never lost it in all those years of
living here, I don't know, maybe he put it on a bit. No, he
never got married, maybe in France, but I don't think so.
He was the classic bachelor type. According to the rumors,
he came to Cataluña with the nationalist army; what can
I say? I really don't know. Then he left and years later he
came back to our city. At the start he knew hardly anyone,
but he was friends or at least he seemed to be on friendly
terms with the Movement's main players in Cataluña and
Valencia. With time he gradually won over the respectable
crowd. Although some of them always kept their distance.
The sort of man who likes to preserve a certain air of mystery, if you see what I mean. There was a rumor that if he

went back to his country he'd have to face a death sentence or a prison term. What had he done to deserve that kind of punishment? Some claimed that he'd collaborated with the Germans, others said he'd killed a child or a number of children, dreadful stories, you know how people love to gossip, and a bit of spite makes it all the more fun. But they ended up accepting him completely. A charming gentleman. How did he earn his living? He gave French lessons. Funny, isn't it? I mean considering how easy it would have been for him to set up a proper business, something more lucrative than a two-bit language school. It's not as if he didn't have money and contacts when he came, I know he did. Maybe it's just that he wasn't intending to stay for so long, who knows?"

GUILLAUME TERZEFF

Paris, 1897–Paris, 1925

"I don't know if I was the first to see him, all I can say for sure is that I was the first to alert the police. It was before six in the morning, and still dark, the only light on the bridge was from the lamps, and that was feeble; I'm used to it, I cross that bridge every day, morning and night, it doesn't bother me. I don't believe in ghosts. It was pretty cold that morning. A bit more than normal, yes, in fact, it was fucking freezing, if you'll pardon my language. Anyway, when I was already more than half way across the bridge I noticed something strange. I mean, it would have been obvious to anyone, that's why I said I didn't know if I was the first to see it. But at that time of day people are often still half asleep, aren't they? Anyhow, there was a rope tied to the balustrade, so I just went to the edge and looked over and saw a body hanging there, two yards below. I crossed myself a couple of times, although I'm not a believer. It was the body of a tall thin young man with long uncombed hair. I knew straight away he was dead. He wasn't moving at all. I mean, the breeze blowing under the bridge was moving the body a bit, but that was all."

Pierre Pain

Paris, 1894–Paris, 1949

"He earned his living reading palms and tarot cards in a cabaret called The House of the Old Companions. That's where I met him and he taught me a part of what I know about the trade. The other part we learned together, Monsieur Pain and I, from the great magician and lord of the night Chu Wei Ku, also known as Daniel Rabinowicz, the quickest pair of hands in all of Europe, the pride of the profession. Tarot, palmistry, Cabalistic mysteries, the enigma of the pyramids, the Chinese horoscope, red magic and black magic, telepathy, reincarnation, Rosicrucianism, numerology, pure rock crystal pyramids, amulets, voodoo, trees of life, we dabbled in every kind of esoteric practice and all of them attracted clients. Even though it was a terrible time in the entertainment business: diabolical years they were, literally diabolical. How did Monsieur Pain come to work there? I guess it was after he lost his war veteran's pension, at the beginning of the Occupation. So it must have been in September, October, or November 1940 that he turned up at the House of the Old Companions looking absolutely pitiful, as if he'd gone for a month without eating so much as a mouthful of bread; Gandhi was plump by comparison. I was fifteen at the time and working as the cabaret's errand boy. A poor orphan with no prospects, starved of affection. I don't know how or why, but before I knew it, the three of us were friends: Chu Wei Ku, who was the star of the show, along with Lita Hoelle, Monsieur Pain and me. Ah, Lita Hoelle! In all my teenage years I never saw a lovelier pair of legs, but most of all she was joyful; she had a true inner joy; when she laughed, it came from her soul, and she made everyone else happy. She must be a grandmother by now; she retired a while back. I bet her grandchildren adore her. Yes, for a while Lita was Chu Wei Ku's lover, but she never knew what we were doing. I guess Chu didn't want to put her at risk, or he didn't trust her, who knows what his reasons were. The group was made up of Chu Wei Ku, Monsieur Pain and myself. No one else. A contact and support group. It was pretty much the same kind of thing as I did for The House of the Old Companions, running errands from A to B. Chu Wei Ku would receive the envelopes and parcels, don't ask me how, and then we shared them out among the three of us, depending on the neighborhood, the time, the nature and the size of the item to be delivered. Quite a pleasant life, really, given the circumstances. Toward the end of 1943, that was when they arrested Chu. Not because of his Resistance work, they never found out about that, but because some pig went and told them that the Chinaman's disguise concealed Daniel Rabinowicz, the Jew. Bad blood and bad luck. In March 1945, at the age of thirty-four, Chu died in a German concentration camp. Some of his numbers will live on in the memories of night owls, revelers, and show-business people, like the fifty disappearing doves reappearing as a hundred, plus another fifty shared among four tables chosen at random. Or the fifteen-year-old boy transformed into an angel, who would then fly away never to be seen again. To cut a long story short, Monsieur Pain and I were left on our own, not knowing what to do, or where to turn in the chaotic struggle against fascism. At first we hoped the Resistance would get in touch with us, but no, nothing, not a word; for the Resistance, or whoever had been sending the messages to Chu Wei Ku, we had ceased to exist. We had no choice but to limit ourselves to the work we were paid to do: Monsieur Pain went on conscientiously reading palms, palms stained with blood, the palms of killers and sinister whores, of spongers and black marketeers, and I went on running errands. By this stage we had no one but each other. When the war was over, we went to work at the Cabaret Panama; the House of the Old Companions was shut down and the owner was jailed for collaboration. Monsieur Pain and I put on some of Chu Wei Ku's old numbers. Then we were at the Carousel, and the Bonnani brothers' circus. That must have been in 47. In any case, a busy routine would have been too much for Monsieur Pain. He tried to get his veteran's pension back, but everything was such a mess in those years; it was hopeless. So we went on working in cabarets and circuses on the outskirts of Paris. Until one day his lungs gave out and he collapsed. He died in my arms, in the manager's office at the Cabaret Madame Doré."